Last-But-Not-Least

LOLA

AND THE WILD CHICKEN

Last-But-Not-Least
LOLA
AND THE WILD CHICKEN

Christine Pakkala   PICTURES BY Paul Hoppe

BOYDS MILLS PRESS
AN IMPRINT OF HIGHLIGHTS
Honesdale, Pennsylvania

Boyds Mills Press

An Imprint of Highlights

815 Church Street

Honesdale, Pennsylvania 18431

Printed in the United States of America

ISBN: 978-1-59078-983-4 (hc) • 978-1-62979-404-4 (pb) • 978-1-62979-278-1 (e-book)

Library of Congress Control Number: 2014935273

First paperback edition, 2015

The text of this book is set in ITC Novarese Std.

The drawings are done in pen on paper, with digital shading.

10 9 8 7 6 5 4 3 2 1

For Michael Pakkala
—CP

For Leokadia
—PH

CONTENTS

1. A JELLY BEAN PLAN

MY NAME IS LOLA ZUCKERMAN,

and Zuckerman means I'm always last. Just like zippers, zoom, and zebras. Last. Zilch, zeroes, and zombies. Last.

ZZZZZZZ when you're too tired to stay awake. ZZZZZZZZ when a bee is about to sting you. Z. Ding-dong LAST in the alphabet.

Every single day my teacher, Mrs. D., lets us out in Alphabetical Order. Every single day my best friend Amanda Anderson zips out the door first, and then Harvey Baxter, Dilly Chang, and Jessie Chavez.

Guess what else? I'll tell you. Every single day Amanda sits with Jessie on the bus going home. Even though they live on the same street and you'd think that would be PLENTY of time to spend together. But NO. You'd be wrong. Dead Wrong.

If only my name were Lola Adventure. Or Lola Amazing. Or Lola Awesome. Even if I were Lola Butterbean or Lola Bowling Ball, I'd beat out Chavez every time. But no. I'm stuckerman with Lola Zuckerman.

BRIIIING!

Mrs. D. says, "Lollipops, time for dismissal," and begins calling our names. Mrs. D. calls us candy names 'cause she luh-huvs candy. Once she got her teeth locked together with caramel.

I wait and wait and wait. I hang off my chair. Past the whole alphabet. Mrs. D. sidles up to me and leans down. She whispers chocolate into my face. "Don't forget to have Mom or Dad sign the permission slip, okay? The field trip is on

Thursday." Then she tucks ANOTHER permission slip into my pocket.

My face heats up and my heart snaps like a rubber band. "My mom and dad went on a trip," I say. "Grandma is taking care of Jack and me until they get back and that's not until Thursday night."

"If Grandma signs it, that will be fine," Mrs. D. whispers.

Whew.

Then she hollers, "Okay, last but not least, Lola, line up."

I skip to the end of the line—*zip*.

"Lola, stop breathing on my neck," Ben Wexler says.

"Lola, take a step back, please," Mrs. D. calls.

Fishsticks! I take a step back.

Mrs. D. leads us out the door. As we walk, I fish around in my candy pocket for jelly beans. My hand sweats on them a little, but I bet they still

taste good. I give one to Ben Wexler.

"Can I trade places?" I ask him. He nods. And I get in front of him. I pass a jelly bean to the new girl, Savannah Travers, and take her place. I work my way up the line, past Timo Toivonen, past Gwendolyn Swanson-Carmichael, past Ruby Snow. All the way up, until I'm behind Jessie Chavez.

"Hey," Jessie says. "You cut."

"Did not. I traded." I hold out a jelly bean. A nice green one. "Wanna trade? I stand in front of you and you get my jelly bean."

Jessie stares at the green jelly bean. Slowly she shakes her head.

"Tell you what," I say. I reach into my pocket and fish out another jelly bean. "I'll make it two." That second jelly bean is a real humdinger. It's a weird one, a double jelly bean. It's pink-pink with tiny bits of light pink. It's all the pink a pink-stinker could want.

Jessie stares at the double jelly bean plus the

green jelly bean. "Fine," she says. "Let's trade." She snatches those jelly beans and—*zloop*—pops the green one in her mouth. She pings the pink one in her pocket.

I squeeze in front of Jessie Chavez and behind Dilly Chang and Harvey Baxter. I can see over them. Straight to Amanda Anderson.

"Hi, Amanda!" I holler-whisper. 'Cause we have to use our inside voices even when we're practically out the door.

Amanda likes The Rules. That's why she doesn't turn around. I bet.

"Amanda! Yoo-hoo!" I yodel-lady-who.

She finally looks at me. Amanda's blue eyes get big and her brown eyebrows pip up. "Lola, what are you doing?!" she says. "You can't cut in line. 'Member?"

"I didn't!" I explain. "I traded my way up."

"Oh!" she says. Then she turns around and—OW OW OW—she smacks right into the closed door

instead of following Mrs. D. through the open one.

She stumbles this way and that way, holding her face.

Mrs. D. whips around. "Amanda, are you okay?"
Mrs. D. hollers it out loud, and I holler it in my
brain.

"I'm fine," she squeaks between her fingers in a Not-Fine-and-It's-Lola's-Fault voice.

"Lola," Mrs. D. barks. "We've already talked about this."

"Okay," I say and slither to the back of the line. Lizards slither and snakes slither and so do kids who have to go all the way to the end of the line. Minus seventeen jelly beans.

Finally, I climb on board Bus One. Sure enough, Jessie and Amanda are nestled in tight like two baby kangaroos in one pouch.

"You always get to sit with Amanda on the way home," I remind Jessie, friendly-like. "Can I sit with her today? Pretty please?"

"No way, José. You're not supposed to get up once you sit down."

That's true. That's one of Sal's bus rules. Also, two to a seat. Not three.

Sal starts up the bus and we plant our tushies and glue our eyes straight ahead. Except I hear a

whistling giggle so I sneak a look around and say,
"What's so funny?"

Amanda shrugs and Jessie shrugs.

"Nothing," Jessie mutters like a toothless
old man.

"Your forehead is purply," I whisper to Amanda. "Does that hurt?" Poor, poor, poor Amanda.

Amanda touches her forehead and squinches up her face. "That's 'cause you distracted me when you cut in line." Uh-oh. She sounds miffed. Miffed is mad but you're not saying.

My heart aches like it walked into double doors and the rest of me doesn't feel good, either. Something's tickling me on the tip of my tongue and I think it's "sorry."

"I'm sorry," I say. "I just wanted to sit with you." I dig out a couple of jelly beans. "Here, Amanda. This'll make you feel better."

I plop the jelly beans in her hand. One is purple like her head and one is black. It turns your teeth black when you chew it. Amanda will love that.

She smiles at me with boring white teeth. "Thanks, Lola!"

Jessie shakes her finger. "You're lucky Amanda didn't get knocked out."

I pop up on my knees and lean over my seat. "You're lucky I don't take back that pink jelly bean."

"No take-backs, Lola Zuckerman," Jessie growls like a vicious Chihuahua.

"Lola!" Sal yells. "We talked about this!"

"Okay!" I plant my tushie double-fast.

Sal zooms down the road. I twist around again. Amanda and Jessie are doing the Hand Jive.

"Can I play?" I ask. Sal drives over a pothole and I bounce into the air.

"You can't play," Jessie says, "'cause you weren't there when we learned it."

"Lola, face forward before you get in trouble," Amanda says.

"I can learn," I say. "I learn fast." I stick my hands in the middle of their Hand Jive.

"OW!" Jessie screams. "You POKED me!"

Our bus whips over to the side of the road. And guess what? It's nobody's stop.

"Lola!" Sal points to me. "Come up here and sit behind me."

I stomp up to the seat where you can count fourteen freckles on Sal's bald head. Where bad kids sit. "Please move over, Harvey," I say.

"Can't."

"Why not?"

"I'm glued to the seat, see?" Harvey grunts and pretends he can't move.

I shove Harvey over and sit down partly on him.

"*Oof!* You crushed me. You weigh more than my dog!"

Harvey is rude like that. He must have missed

school when they had Be-a-Bully-Buster Day.

Sal drives over another pothole and we bounce. Harvey bellows, "Yahoo!"

"Quiet up there!" Jessie Chavez yells.

"Quiet yourself, Jessie!" I holler back.

Sal pulls up to the stop on Windy Hill Drive.

"Bye, Lola," Jessie and Amanda call out at the same time, just like they practiced it.

"Bye," I say, all by my lonesome self.

Amanda pauses at the top of the stairs. "I'll sit with you on the way to school tomorrow."

I smile big as a slice of watermelon. *Whew!* I'm glad Amanda isn't mad at me for distracting her right into the double doors. Amanda waves good-bye and hops—one, two, three—off the bus.

And then I think of something.

I lean over the two teensy kindergarten kids across the aisle. I bang on their window. "AMANDA!" I yell. "AMANDA, WILL YOU SIT WITH ME ON THE FIELD TRIP TO KOOKAMUT FARM?"

But Amanda and Jessie are skipping down Windy Hill Drive.

Amanda can't hear me. Otherwise she'd say yes.

I'll call her soon as I get home. We'll make a plan to sit together on the field trip. We'll pet chickens. We'll learn about harvesting fall crops. We'll pick apples, red for me and yellow for Amanda. We'll get Friend-of-a-Farmer badges. And Jessie can sit with Gwendolyn.

It's the perfect plan.

2. KOOKY BUTT FARM

FINALLY SAL PULLS UP TO MY stop on Cherry Tree Lane, which used to be Amanda's stop, too.

Grandma's waiting for me. She has black hair and red lips and a powdery white face. She looks JUST like Snow White, only old. She's from Brooklyn. She calls Connecticut "Alien Territory." I don't know what she means. There's no one here from outer space.

I hop down the bus steps—one, two, three.

"DARLING! Oh, my DARLING LOLA!" Grandma calls out.

Bang! Bang! I look back and see Harvey pounding on the bus window. "Darling Lola!" he mouths.

Great.

Grandma plants a red lipstick kiss on my head and wraps me up in a perfume hug. It smells like roses in there.

"Hi, Grandma," I say into her arm.

When she finally lets me up for air, I look around. "Where's Patches?" I ask.

"Oh, he's at home, bubelah," Grandma says.

We click-click up Cherry Tree Lane. Grandma swings my arm and sings, "I got apples. I got cherries. I got ice cream. I got my granddaughter. Who could ask for anything more?"

"You could ask for Jack." I point to my brother. He's shooting hoops in the driveway.

"Guess what?" I say. "I'm going on a field trip."

"Oh, how splendid!" Grandma says. "How perfectly divine!"

Jack throws the ball to me but it flies past

and rolls down the driveway. He runs after it. "Where?" he hollers.

"To Kookamut Farm."

"Can I go to Kooky Butt Farm, too?" Jack says, jogging back, jumping up, and tossing the ball into the hoop. Grandma catches it, flings it toward the basket, and it goes right in. She and Jack high-five.

"KOO-KA-MUT," I say. "And no. Only if you're in Mrs. D.'s class."

"Come along, bubelahs," Grandma says. She tucks one arm around me and one around Jack and heads us to the kitchen door.

"I remember that field trip," Jack says. "The teacher brings a big bag of chicken poop to class."

Grandma purses her red lips tight.

I shake my head. "I don't believe you."

"It's true. So that you can get used to the stinky farm smell. *Phlooooo* . . ." Jack makes his mouth fart.

"Jack," Grandma says as she ushers us into the kitchen. "That's hardly the behavior of a gentleman."

"I agree," Jack says.

"Now, Jack, don't give me any guff," Grandma says. "Down, Patches!"

"Grandma, that's how Patches says hello." I give him an extra hug so there's no hard feelings while Grandma pulls something out of the fridge. I can smell it before it even gets here. Maybe it's chilled dog food.

"There you go!" Grandma says. "It's a wonderful whitefish pâté on these simply marvelous onion crackers. A healthy snack for my bubelahs. And

you—" Grandma grabs Patches by the collar and sticks him out on the patio.

"Thanks, Grandma," we say in wet-paper-towel voices.

"I'll be right back," Grandma says. "I need to record *Call of the Humpback Whale* on PBS. Your clever daddy taught me how."

As soon as Grandma's gone, I whisper, "It's weird without Mom and Dad."

"Yeah." Jack looks at the whitefish pâté on onion crackers. "I'll give you Double Pillow Force when we play Blanket of Doom if you eat this."

"Let me see your hands," I say. Last time he gave me Double Pillow Force, he canceled it with Crossies.

He holds up his hands. "No Crossies."

"Fine," I say. I pop two of his whitefish pâté on onion crackers into my mouth and chew them. *BLECH.* Then one more. *GACK.*

Grandma comes clattering back. "Why, Jack. What a WON-derful appetite. Would you like some more, my boychik?"

"Oh, no, I'm full, Grandma," Jack says.

"Say, why don't we harvest those vegetables you and Grandmother Coogan planted?" Grandma says. "Then I can make all kinds of good food for my grandchildren."

I look at Jack.

Jack looks at me.

Grandma's cooking is creative. Mom taught me that word for it. Also: "If you don't have anything nice to say, don't say anything."

I don't have anything nice to say about her Beef Boogy in a Wine Sauce.

I do have something nice to say about the roasted chicken and matzo ball soup Grandma orders from Gottlieb's Restaurant. And about Mom's homemade spaghetti and meatballs even with green flecks.

But I'm not getting any of Mom's good food until Friday.

3. HATCHING CHICKENS

GUESS WHAT? I'LL TELL YOU.
I'm sleeping with the windows wide open.

Here's what happened.

Now, where did that old woman plant those carrots,
Grandma was yelling under her breath. Patches
helped us find some. Then while I called Amanda
and her mom told me that she was at Jessie's,
Grandma made vegetable stew for dinner. But the
turnips wouldn't cook and the carrots cooked too
much and Mom's saltshaker cap fell off right into
all of Grandma's hard work so we ordered from

the Happy Kitchen and Grandma gave Martin, the delivery guy, a big tip.

I talked to Mom on the phone and it sounded like she was downstairs in the kitchen when I was upstairs in my bed. But she wasn't. Then Mom had to say goodbye. It was my bedtime, and Mom was going out to dinner 'cause selling dresses means you have to eat burritos in California.

I didn't even get to talk to Dad at all 'cause he's in Singapore telling somebody how to build a Fancy Man tuxedo store. And that's a whole world away.

So instead I called Amanda's house again to find out if we could sit together on the field trip, but the answering machine told me to leave a message and I didn't want to. I was heartsick until Grandma said we would watch *Call of the Humpback Whale* and drink real herbal tea with loads of honey. She painted my toenails red and Jack had to say sorry for his ball-face lie. They *don't* look like a shark bit them.

Grandma made popcorn in the microwave but

we forgot to listen 'cause the Humpback Whales
were singing. It smoked up the place.

That's why we're sleeping with the windows wide
open.

I like the moon shining straight into my window.
Not Patches. He's howling at it. I wonder if Patches
misses Mom and Dad. Or maybe he's mad at

Amanda's dog for moving away. Or maybe he's heartsick because I am.

Grandma tucks me in. But she doesn't know about a kiss on my forehead and one on each cheek and one on my nose.

"Lola," Grandma whispers at my door. "How would you like to hear a bedtime story?"

My voice scratches out a "Yes, please."

Grandma nestles into my bed. She's got her hair pinned back and white stuff smeared on her cheeks and a scarf wrapped around her neck. She's wearing fuzzy socks and a leopard robe.

"Once there was a chicken. A beautiful fluffy chicken with feathers the color of a Florida orange. And that chicken was named Lola."

I sit up in my bed. "The chicken had my name?"

Grandma nods. "Well, this chicken, Lola, laid an egg. A perfect egg. And so Lola . . ."

"Not me. The chicken," I say and snuggle into my bed and not a chicken's bed.

"Yes, Lola was a lovely chicken and perfect in nearly every way. But she was impatient. She couldn't wait for things to happen. She wanted them to happen *now*. This was a problem for Lola because she needed to sit on the egg and keep it warm so that it would hatch."

"She was a broody hen," I say. "Granny Coogan told me that."

"Yes, indeed, she was. She worried and she worried and she worried. When would the egg hatch? She got off the egg and she called the doctor. The doctor told Lola to sit on the egg."

"Was the doctor a chicken?"

"Yes. Next, Lola went to the scientist and he told her to sit on the egg."

"Was the scientist a chicken, too?"

"No. The scientist was a hound dog. She went to the baker, the dentist, and the teacher."

"Was the teacher Mrs. D.?"

"No, this teacher was a palomino pony. And the

teacher told Lola to be patient. To sit on the egg."

Jack leans around the corner. "What happened?"

I sit up in bed again. "Jack, what are you doing?"

"I want to hear what happens to the egg."

"Come here, boychik," Grandma says, patting the bed. Jack comes in and phlumps on my bed.

"Did the baby chick die?" Jack wants to know.

"Did it?" I ask.

Grandma takes my hand and Jack's hand and gives them each a squeeze. "Lola listened to the advice she was given. She returned to her egg . . ."

"Was it dead? Did a fox steal it?" Jack asks.

"Nooo," Grandma says. "It was still there, waiting for her. So Lola settled herself on her egg."

"Did she smash it by accident?" Jack asks.

"No, she knew just how to sit on it," Grandma

says. "And after . . . a few days . . ."

"Twenty-one days?" Jack says.

"Exactly," Grandma says. "Lola's egg hatched. She had a beautiful chick."

"What did she call it?" I whisper.

"Well, that's a good question, Lola. What do you think she called the chick?"

"Stinker," Jack says.

"Amanda," I say.

Grandma kisses my forehead and huffs out of

my bed. "Off to bed," she says to Jack. "It's past your bedtime, too."

"Way past," Jack says.

"Grandma?"

Grandma pauses at my door. "Yes, Lola?"

"Twenty-one days is a really long time."

"I suppose so," Grandma says.

"Tuesday, Wednesday, and Thursday isn't a long time."

"It's seventy-two hours," Jack says.

"That's a lot of hours," I say.

"It's just enough time for me to spend with my beautiful grandchildren, cooking wonderful food from Grandmother Coogan's vegetable patch. Tomorrow I'm going to make something very special indeed."

"What?"

"You'll have to wait and see."

I don't like waiting and seeing. Me and Lola the Chicken.

4. THE WORLD'S BEST SMOOTHIE

THE NEXT DAY JESSIE CHAVEZ
and Amanda Anderson miss the bus. I see them
running down Windy Hill Road.

"SAL!" I jump up and wave my arms and holler.

"Lola," Sal says. "SIT!"

Fishsticks. I don't get my turn sitting with
Amanda. I don't get to forgive and forget that she
never called me back yesterday.

Maybe it's going to be a bad day.

I'm the first in the classroom, along with our aide
Miss Nimby. I sign up for hot lunch. It's pepperoni

pizza. I sit at my desk and wait for Amanda.

I take out my watermelon-smelling pencil and purple notebook and write:

Why Amanda and I Are Best Friends

1. Amanda tells stories about ghost towns with her black flashlight under her blankets and then you can't sleep in case the Dead Cowboy is coming to get you.

2. Amanda knows real yoga like Down Dogs and she'll teach you if you listen up and stop acting silly.

3. Amanda knows you didn't mean it when your Down Dog crashed into her bookcase and broke her genuine Hummel doll.

The new girl, Savannah Travers, comes in. School started four weeks ago and she just showed up last

Friday 'cause her dad got transferred. She came all the way from California. She's got on her sparkly purple glasses and purple shorts and Goshdango purple cowboy boots with metal tips like real cowboys wear. Savannah luh-huvs purple. She has a picture of her mom taped to the top of her desk. Not me, even though my mom is far away. I wish there were no such thing as California.

"Hi, Lola." She squeaks like a mouse. "Whatcha

doing?" I close my notebook 'cause those are my private thoughts.

"Nothing."

"I like your dress."

"My mom made it. It's a Lola dress. I've got bunches in all different colors."

Savannah looks down at her purple cowboy boots. "My mom bought my boots for me. In California." Her face sags.

Jessie runs into the room. "Missed the bus!" she yells. "My mom drove Amanda and me to school . . ."

"Oh," I say, and my *oh* goes low. Sometimes when Amanda lived next door to me, we missed the bus. My mom would drive us to school so Mrs. Anderson could get to her hot yoga class. Amanda and I would play Miss Mary Mack and holler like there was a fire and Mom couldn't hear NPR. I hope she doesn't play Miss Mary Mack with Jessie or holler like there's a fire. 'Cause Amanda was my friend *first*.

Amanda skips into the room. She's the best

skipper in our class. "Lola-Ba-Mola!" she yells.

"Amanda-Fo-Landa!"

Amanda skips right up to my desk. She's wearing a pink Lola dress. It has a matching pink ribbon and pockets for extra ribbons. It's the perfect Lola dress for Amanda Anderson.

Amanda and I smile our Super Goofer Smiles. Mine is a Pucker Your Lips. Amanda's is a Hang Your

Tongue Out.

"How come you never called me back?"

Amanda talks with her sound turned down. "I went out for Chinese food with Jessie," she says. "And when I got home, it was time for bed." She turns red all over her face. Even her ears turn red, just like my Grampy Coogan's.

"Oh," I say, and that *oh* stands for sad. But at least they didn't go out for Italian. That's my favorite. Italian reminds me of spaghetti and spaghetti reminds me of Mom. And Dad singing "*O sol mio*" when he smells the meatballs.

"I had Chinese food for dinner, too," I tell

Amanda. "Well, first I had vegetable stew. My grandma dug vegetables out of the garden and then we washed the mud off, chopped them up, and cooked rice. But then the salt fell into the stew. So we ordered Chinese food and we also had popcorn. Only we burned the popcorn and the fire alarm went off."

"Fat chance," Jessie Chavez says.

"It's true! My grandma loves to dig up Granny's garden."

"Not that part. The part about the fire alarm," Jessie says.

"Well, yes, sir, it did," I say and my words wobble.

Amanda butts right in. "Do you still have raspberries?" Amanda asks. "Your mom makes really good raspberry smoothies."

"We still have some raspberries," I fib.

"Here's a raspberry for you!" Jessie blows a big one. Little bits of Jessie-spit fly through the air.

"If you keep that up, you're going to the principal's office!" I say. I'd make a good teacher.

The principal's office is where you go to get yelled at. Jessie told me her brother Dustin went about 400 times. He only got out by hip-niptizing the principal. It goes like this: "YOU ARE GETTING SLEEPY. SLEEPY. SLEEPY."

Amanda gives Jessie a glare and slings her arm around me. Jessie's face squishes up and she stomps away.

"Never mind about Jessie," Amanda says. "She says I'm her best friend and I can't talk to you. But I told her all three of us can be best friends."

I'm mad. It feels like a bumblebee is buzzing in my head. *Zzzzz.*

"We'll pick all the fruit in our garden," I say, loud as I can. "We'll make a giant fruit smoothie and we'll drink it up!"

Savannah asks, "Can I have some of the fruit smoothie, too?"

I blink my eyes. Savannah is stuck beside us like a koala hanging onto a eucalyptus tree.

Now Amanda slings her other arm around Savannah. "'Course you can."

"Thank you, Amanda," Savannah says in her whispery voice. "Thank you, Lola."

Why can't that girl speak up?

How can three kids be best friends? Mrs. D. tells us to be problem solvers. I don't want to be best friends with Jessie. And that goes for Savannah, too.

"Amanda!" Jessie says. "We should get a ride to school every day."

Fishsticks.

Then I have the perfect solution.

"Maybe you and Jessie can make smoothies," I tell Savannah.

"I don't like smoothies," Jessie says.

"Me neither," Savannah says in a whispery voice. She slinks past me to her desk and sits down. I feel bad. Ten percent bad and ninety percent not so bad.

"Lola!" Amanda says. "That wasn't nice."

I fold my arms. "Are you having a smoothie or not?"

"Not if you're going to be mean." Amanda stomps away.

"Fine!" I call. "I'm going to make a delicious smoothie and you can't have any. My fruit smoothie is going to taste great! I'm putting in strawberries! Blackberries!

Blueberries! Raspberries! And . . . Regular Old Berries!"

"There's no such thing as Regular Old Berries," Jessie says.

"Yes, sir, there is such a thing," I say.

"Children," Miss Nimby says. "Let's get seated."

"Chugga Chugga Choo!" Harvey Baxter marches around the room. "Climb on board!" he calls. Charlie, Madison, John, and Jessie grab on. "We're the Cool Train!"

"Children," Miss Nimby peeps. "Find your seats."

"You're NOT the Cool Train," Gwendolyn Swanson-Carmichael calls. She already found her seat.

"Come on, Amanda!" Jessie calls. "You're cool, so get on board!"

I cross my arms and glare at Jessie. Glaring is when staring isn't angry enough.

"Let's get settled," Miss Nimby warbles.

Mrs. D. huffs in carrying a huge garbage bag. She drops it with a thud.

"People!" Miss Nimby yells. "Sit down! This is not a three-ring circus!"

The Cool Train runs to their seats. Miss Nimby looks surprised, like she didn't know her voice had a yell setting. Mrs. D. gives Miss Nimby a thumbs-up.

"Sorry I'm late," Mrs. D. says. "But that's no excuse to go wild. All right, Jujubes, time for Share."

We sit on Mrs. D.'s red carpet.

"Who has something to share?" She looks around the circle.

I shoot up my hand. Mrs. D. nods.

"My mom and my dad left," I say. "Now my grandma is watching my brother and me. She makes really rotten food, but she tells really good bedtime stories about chickens."

"Chickens?" Jessie shudders. "Yuck."

"Chickens are not yucky," I say. "Some of them have beautiful orange feathers."

Mrs. D. says, "That's difficult that your parents are traveling. But wonderful that you have a grandmother staying with you." She gives me a Honey Toast smile. "Anyone else want to share?"

Timo Toivonen raises his hand. "Have I told you about Paavo Nurmi? He was a great runner from Finland."

"That's lovely, Timo, but Share is for telling about our own news."

Timo nods. He raises his hand again. "My goldfish died. My father flushed it down the toilet."

"Oh, my. I'm so sorry, Timo." Mrs. D. says.

"I've got three more," he says.

"Any more Shares? No? Okay, Peppermints, class business. Our field trip is this Thursday! For those of you who forgot to turn in permission slips last Friday, please make sure to hand them in today."

Uh-oh. I forgot last Friday, and I can't please make sure to hand mine in today. Because I forgot again.

"I didn't forget last week," Gwendolyn Swanson-Carmichael says.

"Only Lola forgot," Jessie says. "She might miss our super-terrific field trip!"

"No, I forgot, too!" Savannah says. She smiles at me, but I don't want to feel better, so I don't.

"Well, you're new," Jessie tells her. "That doesn't count. You don't know all the rules."

"Jessie," Mrs. D. says in her Cold Coffee voice. "That's enough."

Mom usually signs permission slips and tucks them right into my permission-slip pocket. But not this time. I was supposed to be the big capable kid she knows I am. While she was the busy ol' adult, packing loads of Lola-dress samples into her suitcase.

"Who can tell me the name of the farm?" Mrs. D. asks.

Amanda gives the right answer. "Kookamut Farm!" She brushes some dirt that wasn't even there off her dress.

"Very good. And who can guess what's in this big sack? I'll give you a hint. It has to do with our field trip."

"Ooh, ooh! I know! I know!" Sam says.

"Hand, Sam!" Mrs. D. reminds him. Her lips squinch up. "Let's see—Dilly?"

"Is it seeds?" Dilly peeps.

"Good guess, but no. Lola?"

"Chicken poop," I say loud and clear.

Everyone busts out laughing.

"No," Mrs. D. says. "Now, Lola, let's not get silly."

My face is as hot as Granny Coogan's Four-Alarm Chili.

"What DO I have in the bag?"

Hands shoot up again. But not mine. I will never ever *ever* answer another question.

Mrs. D. calls on Savannah. "Is it chicken feed?" she asks.

"That's right!" Mrs. D. says.

"Hurray!" Amanda calls out. "Hurray for Savannah!"

Humph, I think. Savannah probably cheated. She probably looked through the bag with her ultra-large eyeglasses.

Savannah looks over at me with a smile.

I look back at Savannah. I stick out my tongue.

"Lola!" Mrs. D. hollers.

5. PRINCIPAL MCCOY'S OFFICE OF DOOM

MY TUMMY HURTS. MY EYEBALLS ache. My hands sweat.

I wait in the office with Mrs. Crowley, the secretary. Kids call her Mrs. Growly because she never smiles. Sure enough, she's never smiling now. I'm also not smiling. I'm staring at an inkblot on the carpet. Who spilled the ink? Now THAT'S a bad kid.

Finally, Principal McCoy comes out of his office. His arm is STILL in a sling from when he wiped out in the cafeteria a couple of weeks ago.

"Hello, Lola."

I open my mouth to say something. But it feels like peanut butter in there. We shake hands and it's a good thing his left hand is the one in the sling.

He points to his office. It says Princi-PAL on the door.

"Come with me, Lola."

I follow him. He points to a fluffy orange chair. I sit on it. It feels like resting on the tummy of a fat orange cat. Maybe the chair has secret claws.

Principal McCoy gets behind his desk. "So, Lola, what seems to be the problem?"

"You are getting sleepy. SLEEPY. SLEEPY," I say.

But Principal McCoy looks wide awake. "Lola?" he asks. "What's going on?"

Now I feel like a basketball is stuck in my throat. "Are you going to scream at me?"

"Lola! Whatever gave you that idea? Of course not."

I take a deep breath. I sink down in the fluffy orange chair.

"Tell me what happened in class."

"I read that snakes taste the air by sticking out their tongues. Like thith." I show him.

Principal McCoy sticks his tongue out at me. "Like that?"

"Yeah."

"So you wanted to try that?"

My tongue droops. "Yeth."

"You weren't sticking your tongue out at Savannah Travers?"

I can see what he means. "Sort of."

"Oh. And how do you think that made her feel?"

"Bad."

"How do you think you can solve the problem?" Principal McCoy sounds like Mrs. D. Maybe they went to Problem Solvers School together.

"I could tell her I'm sorry I tasted the air in her direction. I mean . . . stuck my tongue out."

Principal McCoy stands up. "That sounds like a plan! All right, Lola!" He looks at his watch. "Your class is now at recess."

Principal McCoy and I shake hands again.

"By the way, guess what? This isn't the only bad thing that happened to me," I tell him.

"Oh, really?"

"Yep. My mom and dad left."

"Oh, gee." Principal McCoy says "oh gee" a few more times.

6. BIG MESS AT RECESS

I MARCH RIGHT OVER TO JESSIE
Chavez. She's hanging off the monkey bars.

"Hi, Lola," she says, upside-down. "Did you get yelled at?"

"No. Principal McCoy let me sit in his cat seat. You were wrong."

Jessie's face looks happy. Except she's upside-down. So I guess it looks sad. "Sorry," she says in a sorry-but-not-really voice.

"Where's Savannah?" I say in my I-heard-you-but-I-don't-forgive-you voice.

She points to the swings. "Hogging Amanda,"
she says. "But it's more fun hanging on these super-
deluxe monkey bars. You should try."

"No, thanks." And I march over to the swings
and as I'm marching Jessie runs by me. So I start
running, too. Jessie and I race to the swings. I win
and stop in front of Amanda. "Hi, Amanda!" I call.

"Hi, Lola!" she sings out.

"Hi, Savannah!" I say. I'm warming up to sorry.

Savannah swings right on by. That Savannah swinger is swinging and singing. Amanda is singing, too.

"We're the swingers, we're the swinging singers, the ding-a-ling swinger singers," they sing. 'Cause Amanda's really good at making up fun songs.

The bell rings and Jessie yells, "Come on, Amanda! Let's get in line!" She tries to wedge me out of the way so she can stand directly in front of Amanda.

"I was here first," I hiss at Jessie like a mean ol' rattlesnake. And I dig my feet into the dirt. 'Cause I forgot that I came over to say sorry to Savannah for sticking out my tongue. Now I think I came over to fight with Jessie.

"So?" she says. "It's not private property, Lola! Come on, Amanda!" She shoves me out of the way. I lose my balance and grab her arm and we both go TIMBER! I fall to the ground. *WHOMP!* She goes straight into Savannah.

THWACK! Savannah's purple Goshdango metal-tipped cowboy boots kick Jessie right in the chin. Savannah's sparkly purple glasses land next to me and then Savannah warbles, "My glasses!" She jumps out of her swing and—*CRUNCH*—steps right on them.

Amanda Anderson plants her feet on the ground and stops. "LOLA ZUCKERMAN!" she yells. "JUST LOOK WHAT YOU DID!"

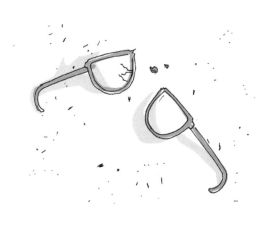

7. THIS MIGHT STING A LOT

I PERCH ON THE HIGH-UP TABLE in the nurse's office. Jessie and Savannah sit there, too. Savannah is holding a little plastic baggy that has her sparkly purple glasses. Now one of the lenses looks like a spider web.

"Jessie!" Nurse Ramirez says. "If you don't stop screaming, I won't be able to clean you off."

"IT HURTS! IT HURTS REALLY BAD!" Jessie yells. "LOLA SHOVED ME! SAVANNAH KICKED ME!"

"No, sir, I never did," I say. "You pushed me and I fell down."

Nurse Ramirez has her hands full. That's what she keeps saying: "Boy oh boy, I've got my hands full." Now she mutters, "I think she's going to need stitches." Mutter is when you whisper with spit in your mouth.

"STITCHES!" Jessie cries. "*WAH! WAAAAH!*"

"Hold still, Jessie!" Nurse Ramirez says sternly. "I won't know if you need stitches until I clean you off. Maybe you don't."

Jessie quiets down. Nurse Ramirez soaks a gauze pad with cleaner. She swipes it across Jessie's chin.

"OW! OWOWOWOWOW!" Jessie yells. "That stings!"

"Okay, okay," Nurse Ramirez says in a bedtime voice. She pats Jessie on the back.

Nurse Ramirez cleans off all the blood. There's a gross cut underneath. Savannah squints. Lucky for her, she can't see without her sparkly purple glasses. She can't see Jessie's chin.

Jessie's lips go wobbly.

"Okay, then," Nurse Ramirez says loudly. "Let's get a butterfly bandage on this to close it up."

A lady in a pink velvet outfit jogs old-people-style into the room.

"Bammy!" Jessie cries.

"Oh, my poor Jessiekins!"

I look at Savannah. Savannah looks at me. It's sad that Jessie is hurt. But it's funny that Jessie is Jessiekins.

"How did this happen?!" Jessie's grandma ask-yells at Nurse Ramirez.

"A playground accident," Nurse Ramirez explains. "Here are directions to the emergency room." She sticks the paper in Jessie's grandma's hand.

My face locks down. Is this all my fault? I wish I was the one with the cut. Then it wouldn't be my fault.

"I swung into her, ma'am," Savannah says in her soft voice.

"Well, that wasn't very nice, was it?" Jessie's grandma says in a you-already-know-the-answer way.

Poor Savannah. Her eyes water up. "I want my mom," she squeaks like a baby koala.

Jessie says, "It's not your fault, Savannah. It's yours, Lola Zuckerman! You got in my way!"

"Now, now," Jessie's grandma says. "Let's not get upset." But then she shoots me a Death Glare. "We'll let your teacher handle this, Jessiekins."

And they march right out the door.

Oh, boy.

Nurse Ramirez pats Savannah and me on our heads. "Toots, we'll have to be a little more careful, that's all," she says to Savannah. "And no more standing close to the swings," she says to me. I nod my head up and down so hard my brains scramble around.

"Now, what hurts?" Nurse Ramirez asks us.

"You first," Savannah tremble-says.

"No, you first," I say. I smile with all my teeth.

"Okay. My ankle hurts." Savannah puts down her sparkly-purple-glasses baggy and takes off a boot. "My glasses came off and then I jumped out of the swing and my ankle twisted."

"Can you stand on it?" Nurse Ramirez asks.

Savannah stands. "Now it doesn't hurt," she says.

Nurse Ramirez helps her back up on the high bed. "I don't think it's broken or sprained, but we'll wrap it up just to be safe." She takes a big bandage and wraps it around Savannah's ankle. "And here's an ice pack for it."

I say, "You look like a mummy." I smile so Savannah knows I mean a nice mummy.

Savannah sticks her arms out. "I am coming to get you," she moans in a mummy voice.

I laugh it up big, bigger than normal.

"What happened to you?" Nurse Ramirez asks.

"Jessie knocked me to the ground."

"Does anything hurt?"

"Just my feelings because I was standing there trying to say sorry to Savannah and Jessie shoved me and . . ."

"All right. I'll be right back," Nurse Ramirez says. "I need to get forms for you two to bring to your teacher."

As soon as she leaves, I say, "Savannah, I'm sorry I stuck my tongue out at you."

"That's okay, Lola."

Savannah takes off the ice pack. I spy sideways at her. "Want to play hot potato, only frozen potato?"

"Yep," Savannah says.

She tosses me the ice pack, and I throw it back to her. Back, forth, back, forth.

Nurse Ramirez comes in with the forms. "Well, it looks like you're both well enough to return to

class." She hands us each a form. "Make sure you give these to Mrs. D. And I'll be calling your moms and dads to let them know about the accident."

Suddenly Savannah starts to cry. First she cries a little. Then a lot.

8. 66 ¾ HOURS

"WHAT HURTS?" NURSE RAMIREZ
asks. "Your ankle?"

"I want my mom!" Savannah yowls.

"You'll get to see her in three and a half hours," I
say, trying to keep the grouch out of my voice. "See
the clock?"

"I can't see anything without my glasses. And
I still can't tell time," Savannah says through her
tears. "And even if I could, I still wouldn't get to see
her. She's in California. She's packing up our old
house. She won't be here until tomorrow."

"My mom's in California, too. I won't get to see her until Friday morning, because she's coming home way after my bedtime on Thursday night."

Savannah sniffs. "She is?"

"Yep."

"Poor you. Are you sad?"

I sit up straight and stick out my chin. I don't need Savannah Travers feeling sorry for *me*! "I can tell time. I can tell when she's going to be home." I look at the clock. "She's going to be home in 67 hours."

Savannah's mouth drops open. "That's a LOT of hours."

I feel my lips puckering. But not for a kiss.

"No, sir. I'll be sleeping for a bunch of them. And I'll be on the Kookamut field trip for five of them."

"Nurse Ramirez," someone calls over the intercom. "Kindergartener down in the cafeteria!"

She grabs her black bag. "Gotta go. Come along, kids. Lola, can you make sure Savannah gets back to class safely?"

"Sure." I tuck my arm in Savannah's. She picks up her sparkly-purple-glasses baggy and we walk down the hall. At Mrs. D.'s classroom, I look at the clock.

Still 66 and ¾ hours to go. For me.

Only one more day for Savannah.

She's lucky. She gets to wear a mummy bandage and she gets her mom and Amanda Anderson isn't mad at her even though Savannah kicked Jessie right in the chin with her metal-tipped, ultra-pointy purple cowboy boots.

Fishsticks. Some of me likes Savannah and some of me doesn't, and the some of me that doesn't is arm-wrestling the some of me that does.

9. THE WORST PERSON ON PLANET EARTH

IT'S QUIET READING TIME BACK in the classroom. Everybody stares when we walk in. Except Amanda Anderson. She glares and grimaces. Her name should be Grimanda Growlerson.

"Girls, where's Jessie?" Mrs. D. asks.

"Jessie went to the emergency room," I explain and hand her the nurse forms. "She's getting stitches."

"Cool!" Ari Shapiro says. "One time my brother got five stitches. He walked into my sword."

"My sister broke her arm once," Ruby Snow says.

"She fell out of our tree fort."

Mrs. D. makes a shuddering sound. "How awful."
She looks at the forms and then at Savannah.
"Where are your glasses, dear?"

Savannah holds up the baggy of glasses and
squeaks something. So I say, "She broke them."

Amanda looks over her book, *Princess Power*. "YOU
broke her glasses!" she yells

out from a
beanbag on
the floor.

"I DID NOT!"
I yell back.

"You did, too!
You shoved
Jessie right
in front of
Savannah."

"No, I didn't,"
I say. "I never

did that. She shoved me! Then I fell over. And I
grabbed hold of her. And . . ."

And that's mean of Amanda to say because
sometimes I'm lying about being bad, but this time
I'm not. I didn't mean to fall down.

"Why can't you be nice, Lola Zuckerman?"
Amanda says.

"I AM nice," I say.

"Not to Savannah. And not to Jessie."

"Amanda! Lola! That's enough! What has gotten into you two?"

Amanda goes back to reading her book. Her face pinks up. I blink my eyes, one, two, three times.

Savannah squints out at the class.

"Is your book on your desk? I'll get it for you," I tell her, extra loudly so that Amanda can hear how helpful I'm being. And then she'll believe me. We'll be best friends again, and I'll have a sleepover at her house. After we go out for Italian food, she'll tell me haunted stories of the Wild West, and we'll watch *Cupcake Queens* because being a friend means doing boring stuff the other person likes some of the time. And we will only paint our fingernails with adult supervision.

I rush over to Savannah's desk and give her *Your Pet Gerbil*.

Then I hurry back to my desk and open my book.

But every time the story gets good, I think about poor Jessie getting stitches. I wonder if they use a sewing machine like Mom's.

"Quiet reading time is over," Mrs. D. says. "Time to find your seats and take out your Kookamut Farm vocabulary sheet. Oh, Lola, come up here, please."

I go up there even though I want to keep walking

past her desk and right out the door.

"Lola," Mrs. D. says. "Is there anything you want to tell me about the playground incident?" Mrs. D. looks right at me through her rectangles.

My knees sweat in the back. "Nope."

"Nothing at all?"

I'm sure she wants me to tell her something and I'm sure I don't want to. It's a tug-of-war. Her eyebrows are stuck in *I think you'd better* and my face is frozen in *No thanks*.

She keeps looking at me.

My eyeballs swing this-a-way and that-a-way.

"Okay," she says, and I know

I've won. She slides an envelope across her desk.
"Would you please give this to your grandmother?"
I take it. Maybe I haven't won after all.

10. A (NOT VERY) BRIGHT IDEA

I SEE GRANDMA THROUGH THE bus window. She's got a big smile on her face. It's a few teeth past happy.

"Lola!" Grandma cries when I step off the bus. "Are you okay, bubelah? The school called to say you'd had a minor accident."

"I'm fine, Grandma," I say, and I shake all my parts so she can see.

"They assured me you weren't injured, but how I worried, Lola! I was simply frantic."

The note from Mrs. D. crinkles in my pocket. When I give her the note, it will really ruin her day. She'll know I'm a *zhlub*. That's Jewish for bozo. Maybe I'd better not give it to her.

Grandma holds my hand tight as we walk home. It's a big mess in the backyard. Jack is shoveling. Dirt is flying everywhere. Jack loves a chance to go crazy.

Jack steps on his shovel. He's got a big load of dirt. He doesn't notice Grandma, squatting down to pull up a weed. Jack throws it over his shoulder.

Splat! Right on Grandma's neck.

"Jack!" Grandma yells. "Why on earth are you digging holes?" She takes a deep breath. "Please don't do that."

"Sorry, Grandma," Jack says.

Grandma stands up and brushes herself off. "Jack, it's bad enough that Patches is digging holes."

"But he dug up some carrots," Jack tells us.

"That's a good dog," I say and pat Patches on the back. He wags his tail.

"I'm going inside to change my shirt," Grandma says. "I'll be right back."

After Grandma goes inside, I get a bright idea.

"You dug a nice-looking hole there," I say.

Jack looks down. "Yep."

I hold up the envelope. *Mrs. Zelda Zuckerman*, it says. Jack opens his eyes wide.

"I'll do it, but it will cost you," Jack says.

"What?"

"Whatever Grandma's making for dinner tonight—you have to be the one to take seconds when Grandma says if we really loved her food, we'd take seconds."

"That's not fair!"

"She'll be back soon. Make up your mind."

"Fine." I point to the hole. Jack nods. I toss the note in and Jack dumps a big load of dirt on top.

Jack and I give each other a high five. After a while Grandma comes clattering out and Patches scampers over. He tries to dig up the note but we give him a big dog hug. "It's nice to see you two getting along," she says. "My sister and I are the best of friends."

Patches barks and barks. He wants that note. Luckily, Grandma doesn't speak dog.

"Lola, go change," Grandma says. "Then come right out. I want to get these vegetables harvested before sundown."

I run up to my room. I take off my Lola dress and put on shorts and a T-shirt. Outside, Grandma is reading a cookbook. She has a stack of books on the picnic table—more cookbooks, gardening books, and regular old books. Jack is lying flat on his back in the grass.

"How come you're not helping?" I ask.

"I'm guarding Patches," Jack says.

"We're going to have wonderful turnip soup," Grandma says. She hands me a spade.

"Turnips grow wild in Siberia," I tell her.

"I grow wild in Connecticut," Jack says.

I look at the spade. "Grandma, what do I do?"

Grandma says, "Find the turnips and dig them out." She opens up a gardening book and flips through the pages. "Yes. That's it." She points. "See that row of green tops? Those are the leaves of the baby turnips. Dig them out. But be careful not to hurt them."

I kneel down and dig out each one of the baby turnips. They are tiny and white with green feathery leaves.

"Good girl, Lola! We can even eat the top part
of the turnips. See here?" She points to the page
in her gardening book. "It's high in vitamin C. Now,
over there we've got a row of eggplant. Tomorrow
night I'll make eggplant parmesan."

I go to work on the eggplants. Jack and I give
each other the talk-look. It says, "Do you remember

the last time she made eggplant parmesan?" It also says, "We fed it to Patches and he got the runs."

●●●

At night, Dad calls us and guess what? It's already tomorrow in Singapore. Dad is having oatmeal and black coffee at his hotel and I haven't even gone to bed! Then we call Mom and her voice sounds busy. Grandma tucks me in. And she still

94

doesn't know about fluffing my pillow. Or about a kiss on my forehead and one on each cheek and one on my nose.

Grandma tells me another story about Lola the Chicken. This one is about Lola the Chicken traveling to Brooklyn to visit her Grandma and enjoying some of the exciting places that Brooklyn has to offer. Not to mention getting to eat all the ice cream you can hold at Gottlieb's.

Grandma shuts off my light. Then she says in the dark, "Oh, Lola. Mrs. DeBenedetti called me."

"She did?" I feel all sweaty.

"She said she sent you home with an extra copy of the permission slip. Do you have that permission slip for me, Lola?"

Fishsticks.

"Oh, never mind, dear," Grandma says with a yawn. "We'll take care of it in the morning. We wouldn't want you to miss that field trip. It sounds simply wonderful!"

11. DIGGING IN THE DARK

RING! MY FUZZY PETE THE SHEEP
alarm goes off. I shut it fast before Grandma wakes
up. She wouldn't like it if she woke up without
coffee and a bran muffin—and morning. 'Cause it's
midnight.

Slurp! Slurp!

"Patches—get off me! Patches!" I groan.

Slurp! Slurp!

"Okay, I'm up, I'm up."

I roll out of bed. It's black-dark in my room and
brown-dark outside. I get out my mini flashlight

and squish my feet into my sneakers. I tiptoe down the hall. Patches goes into the bathroom. He drinks from the toilet. "Patches, get out of there!" I whisper.

Now comes the scary part. Downstairs. In the dark.

The kitchen is shadowy and spooky. The coffeepot looks like a little goblin sitting on the counter.

"I know, I know," I tell Patches. "It's scary. But it's okay, I'll protect you."

I run past the coffee goblin and so does Patches.

Opening the back door, I tiptoe out to the garden, Patches at my heels. The moon helps me see a little. And so does my mini flashlight. But all the rows in the garden look exactly alike. Where did Jack and I plant that note? Then I remember! It was somewhere near the baby turnips. I grab my spade from the picnic table where I didn't put it away and that's no way to take care of your gardening tools.

I dig a hole. No note. I dig another hole. No note. I dig and dig and dig. And finally I find the note.

"Presto," I say.

Just then, Patches takes off running across the yard.

"Patches, no!" I whisper as loud as a whisper can go. "Come back here, Patches! Leave that squirrel alone."

The poor squirrel probably thought it was safe to walk around the yard at night.

Patches runs this way and that way. I jump when he runs by. I catch him by the tail. He lets out a howl. I grab him by the collar.

"That will be enough!" I march Patches into the kitchen. "You lie down right now!"

Suddenly all the lights turn on.

Grandma stands there, holding Jack's hockey stick. "Lola!" she yowls.

"Hi, Grandma." I hang my head. And that makes me see that I'm covered with dirt from knee to toe.

"What in the world are you doing up at . . ."

She looks across the room at the kitchen clock.

"Midnight," I say.

"And . . . ?"

"I buried the permission slip when we were digging."

"Lola, why?" Grandma asks.

Why gets stuck in my throat.

I cough it out. "I thought it would say I was bad because I stuck my tongue out at Savannah and I got sent to Principal McCoy's office."

"Lola, you didn't need to bury anything! I knew about your trip to the principal's office." Grandma sighs. "And the playground accident. Lola, you don't have to keep secrets from me."

"I'm sorry, Grandma," I say. "I won't anymore."

Except it's a tiny fib. Because I can't tell Grandma that she's a terrible cook.

12. REGULAR BERRIES

AMANDA ANDERSON WON'T LOOK at me. She won't talk to me. I'm see-through, like hot stinky Patches breath. She stomps past me on the bus and squeezes in tight with Jessie Goat Gruff who has stitches under the bandage on her chin.

Jessie won't talk to me, either. I can't say, "You were shoving me, too!"

Because she's the one with the stitches, not me. She's got the right of way.

When we get to school, Amanda skips into Mrs. D.'s class, holding hands with Jessie.

"Oh, my heavens!" Mrs. D. exclaims. "Oh, Jessie! You poor thing!" She cozies right up to Jessie and kneels down in front of her. A whole bunch of kids crowd around, too.

I slink in like an old raccoon that's heading for the garbage cans. I slap my permission slip in Mrs. D.'s basket and slug over to my desk.

What if I were the one with stitches all over my face? And a broken leg? The whole entire school would be weeping and carrying on 'cause I just about killed myself on the playground.

I have a little smile on my face. Until Mrs. D. calls, "Lola, time for morning Share!"

I see that everyone is sitting on the carpet. I skunk on over there.

"Here, Lola!" Savannah says. She pats the seat next to her. She is wearing sparkly blue glasses. Why is Savannah so nice? I wouldn't be nice to me.

But I sit down next to her anyway. "I like your new glasses," I tell her.

"They're my spare pair."

Amanda could think of a good song to go with that. *We're the spare pair, the double-daring spare pair. Not some old underwear.*

Well, better than that. I give Amanda a little wave but I'm still see-through.

"Who would like to share?" Mrs. D. asks.

Gwendolyn Swanson-Carmichael's hand shoots up like a rocket. So does Savannah's.

But Gwendolyn starts talking. "I have something important to say. My mother is picking me up after school for a special trip to New York City. We're having dinner with my father at Tavern on the Green."

My head sinks so I use my fist to prop it up. I stare as hard as I can at Harvey's shoe, which has a wad of gum stuck to the bottom. I swallow some air and hiccup. I haven't seen my mom for a

hundred years. Or my dad.

"How wonderful, Gwendolyn," Mrs. D. says. "Savannah?"

Savannah has her arm flapping in the breeze. I feel her big eyes on me from behind her spare pair. Her arm falls down.

"Um . . . I forgot," she says.

Jessie's hand pops up. "I went to the emergency room and got stitches," she says. "My doctor said I was very brave."

"They always say that," Harvey says.

"I'm sure you were brave," Mrs. D. says. "Any more Shares?"

There are more Shares. Loads more.

But I don't have anything to share, so I just keep my mouth shut.

Finally it's time for Writing Workshop. I get out my purple

notebook and my watermelon-smelling pencil and I write a story:

Once upon a time there were two puppies who were best friends. Then an old skunk came along and tried to squirt the puppies. And a koala came along and tried to hang on to them. But the puppies ran away and left the skunk and the koala alone to squirt and hang on to each other.

By the way, the puppies were named Amanda and Lola.

The End.

We have math and Spanish and then it's time for recess.

"Savannah, be careful with your glasses," Mrs. D. says. "Your mother called to say that they are your only extra pair." Mrs. D. gives Savannah a Sugar Bun

smile. "And I'm sure you're very glad to have her back, aren't you?"

Savannah nods her head like a Savannah Bobblehead. And I am Mom-sick and I can't even remember what she looks like. What if she decides to stay in California forever? What if she's got on some purple cowboy boots and she's sitting on a palomino pony and she never wants to come back? What if every kid in California wants a Lola dress and Mom has to stay and make them?

Mrs. D. calls us in alphabetical order. Except she skips over Jessie and me.

The class and Miss Nimby head out for recess. Mrs. D., Jessie, and I stay put.

Jessie raises her hand. "Am I in trouble?" she asks. "Or are you looking out for my chin?"

"Come here, girls," Mrs. D. says.

We go up there.

"Who would like to explain what happened on the playground at recess yesterday?"

"I'm the one with stitches," Jessie quivers. "Tell Lola to explain. It's all her fault."

"It is not! I was there first, trying to say sorry to Savannah. And you shoved me. You made me lose my balance."

"You didn't have to grab me!"

"I didn't mean to."

"But I got hurt!"

"Well, so did I. On the inside."

"Jessie, is it true that you pushed Lola?"

Jessie folds her arms tight. "Well, maybe. It's Savannah's fault for swinging with sharp cowboy boots."

"What do you have to say to each other?" Mrs. D. says.

"Watch where you're going?" I ask.

"Try again, Lola."

"Sorry, Jessie," I say.

"Sorry, Lola," she says. Then, "You're lucky you didn't get stitches," Jessie adds on to her I'm-not-sorry sorry.

"You're lucky the whole class doesn't blame you, including your own best friend that you've had your whole life."

"My stitches hurt," she says.

Mrs. D. stands up with her travel mug. "Let's go to Nurse Ramirez's office and get you some ointment. Lola, you may now join the class for recess."

They wheel out of the room. But I stand there sputtering like Grampy Coogan's lawnmower. I go over to the window. Fishsticks. There's Savannah swinging Double Dippers with Amanda.

This whole mess is Savannah's fault. She's the best-friend-hogger. She's the Spare-Pair-Wearer and Pointy-Purple-Boot-Attacker. Now Amanda thinks I'm bad. Maybe I AM bad.

I walk over to Savannah's desk and look at the picture of Savannah's mother taped there. She still has a photo, even though her mom got out of California. My mom's stuck there.

Maybe she likes it there better. Maybe she's getting a golden tan and she's surfing.

Maybe the girls there are nice and whispery like Savannah and don't have to be told twice to clear the table.

Now Savannah has her mom back. And I still don't have my mom back. Or my dad.

Picking up a fat black pen, I give her mom glasses, just like Savannah's. Plus, a fat mustache under the mom's nose. Dot, dot, dot: freckles.

All the air squelches out of me. I drop the pen and run out of the room.

13. LOLA STINKERMAN

WHY DID I DO THAT? WHY OH WHY
oh why oh?

I'm the worst, most mean person in the world.

I have to go back in there and get rid of that
picture.

I turn around to go back in the room, but Mrs.
Sweeney, the reading specialist, yoo-hoos me out
to the playground. Fishsticks.

As soon as I get out to the playground, Savannah
runs straight up to me.

"Wanna swing Double Dippers?" she asks.

"Um, maybe later," I tell her purple sneakers 'cause no way am I going to look right at her and show off what a ball-face liar and rotten stinkerman I am.

One of her purple boots kicks a rock. "Okay," she says.

And she runs off.

All during recess, I stay far away from Amanda and Savannah and Jessie, when she comes out with her chin greased up. I keep my eyes fixed on the door for when Mrs. D. hollers for us to line up. I'll have to use magical powers on her or something so she lets me go into the classroom first.

"LOLA! Get over here!" Gwendolyn yells. She, Ruby Snow, and Rita Rohan are sitting on the hopscotch square.

I scoot on over, keeping one eye on them and one eye on the door.

"It's time for the Girl Power Club meeting," Ruby reminds me.

Gwendolyn looks at me with a scowl. "You can't be president today, Lola Zuckerman."

I fold my arms up real tight. "Why not?"

"'Cause we don't want you to give us stitches."

"I didn't give Jessie stitches. The doctor did."

"You know what I mean," Gwendolyn says. "You gave her the cut and THAT gave her stitches."

"I did NOT give her the cut," I say. "Savannah's pointy-toe boot did." That reminds me to look at the door. Mrs. D. didn't come out yet.

"A) You pushed Jessie. Therefore, B) she ran into Savannah's foot. Therefore, C) she got stitches," Gwendolyn says.

"Could she be the secretary?" Ruby asks.

Gwendolyn thinks for a minute. "Okay," she finally agrees. "You have to write down everything we say at the meeting."

"But I don't have anything to write with," I say. I look at the door again because that might be more interesting than writing down everything Gwendolyn Swanson-Carmichael has to say.

"Then you'll have to memorize what we say."

That doesn't sound very fun. But I don't say anything, 'cause I've already got loads of kids mad at me.

Guess what? It's not fun. My brain runs out of room right after Gwendolyn calls the meeting to order. I have some opinions, but I'm supposed to just listen and not talk and that sounds a lot like school.

My brain gets sleepy and I forget to pay attention.

The bell rings. *Oh, the bell just rang*, I think. Then I think, *THE BELL JUST RANG!* I have to get that picture before Savannah sees it!

I run to the front of the line. "I have to cut in line," I tell Jessie. "I have an emergency."

"Lola Z-for-Zuckerman, get to the END OF THE LINE!" Jessie hollers.

"But, but, but—"

"Motor boat, motor boat, zoom away," Harvey Baxter chants.

Mrs. D. opens the door. Her face looks like she accidentally ate a Hot Attack Mouth Whack candy when she expected to eat a Jeffrey Yum Sugar Bun.

"LOLA!" she barks.

But instead of sending me back to the end of the line where I really wish I was, and where I never ever want to get out of again, Mrs. D. hustles me right past Amanda Anderson.

"Miss Nimby, please stay with the children," Mrs. D. says. Then she hurries my I-want-to-go-slow feet down the hall and into the classroom. She shuts the door.

I am throwing up inside my stomach. She holds up the picture of Savannah's mom that looks like a business guy.

"Did you do this?" Mrs. D. says in the world's quietest voice.

I hang my head because it weighs a whole lot. "Yes, Mrs. D."

"Oh, Lola," Mrs. D. says. "Why?"

"I had a rotten moment," I whisper. "But I wished I could erase it. But I couldn't."

"This is a very big problem, Lola," Mrs. D. says.

"What are you going to do about it?"

"Tell Savannah I'm sorry? Because I am."

"That's a start, Lola. Have you ever heard the expression, 'Actions speak louder than words'?"

I nod, except that's a tiny fib.

"Maybe showing Savannah you're sorry will be better than only telling Savannah you're sorry."

"I should only show her?"

"You'll want to find a way to do both, I think. Meanwhile, Lola, I'm going to put this picture in my desk. We're not going to show this to Savannah or talk about it now, so that Savannah won't be upset by it."

I nod up and down, up and down. Good old Mrs. D. That's what I would do if I were the teacher.

"And you are going to visit Principal McCoy again. Do we understand each other?"

"Yes," I whisper. Because now I understand her. And I don't want to be a teacher anymore.

She puts the photo in her desk and lets in the rest of the class.

"What happened, Lola?" Harvey asks. "What did you do now?"

"That's enough, Harvey," Mrs. D. says in her Strike Three voice.

And guess what? That is only Part One of Bad. Part Two of Bad is right around the bend.

14. PART TWO OF BAD

SQUAWK.

It's Savannah. Her *squeak* became a *SQUAWK*.

"Where'd the p-p-p-p-picture of m-m-m-my m-m-m-mom go?"

My whole body turns red.

Savannah's lower lip tucks in. Behind her spare glasses, I can see her eyes up close. They are getting wettish.

Mrs. D. rushes over. "Savannah, dear! Something happened and your photo was ruined, but don't worry! I called your father. He said he had an extra copy and that you could bring it tomorrow." She gives Savannah her Cinnamon Roll smile. Warm and sweet.

I wrap my arm around Savannah. "You okay?" I ask in a Mommy voice. Because she doesn't know I'm the something that happened to her photo.

Savannah nods.

But Mrs. D. gives me the Lime Popsicle look. Cold and sour. "You know what to do next, Lola," she says.

I am going to the principal's office again. On my way, I pass my own desk. Something is taped to it. An envelope. It says:

Lola,

Please deliver to Mrs. Zelda Zuckerman. Have her sign it and return it. I need it before our field trip.

Mrs. DeBenedetti

That seems like the worst part of bad. But the other worst part of bad is Savannah.

At the end of the day, Savannah slips a packet of

jelly beans in my hand. "Those are from California," she says. "When you miss your mom, you can eat one of those and feel better."

If I did eat one, I just might be the saddest bad girl in the whole world.

15. A ROTTEN TOMATO

Dear Mrs. Zuckerman,

Your granddaughter is NOT ALLOWED on our class field trip. She is a rotten tomato. She's a real stinker. She drew all over Savannah's picture of her mom. Even though Savannah is her friend now. Please send her to prison. She needs to learn manners.

Also, she's not the Number One Granddaughter like you said. Not by a long shot.

Sincerely,

Mrs. D.

Well, I haven't actually read the note. But if I do read it, it will say that.

Lucky for me Grandma is TOO busy singing to read it. I hand it over to her, and she sticks it in her pocket and swings my arm.

"I've got a girl named Lola! Don't want to boast, but I know she's the toast of Cloverdale." Grandma croons and then she pulls me up the street. Click, jog, click, jog. "We've got to hurry, Lola," Grandma puffs. "I've got all SORTS of tasty things cooking for dinner tonight."

Patches is sitting outside on the patio and Jack is shooting baskets in the driveway.

"Come in, Jack," Grandma calls. "It's time for your after-school snack! You can't go to soccer practice hungry."

"Aw, Grandma," Jack says. "I'm still not hungry."

"Nonsense!" Grandma says in her I-mean-it voice. "A growing boy needs nutrition."

Jack and I trudge into the kitchen and plop.

"I'll give you Double Pillow Force . . ."

"No way, José," I say.

Grandma comes dancing to the table with dead thumbs pronged into eyeballs and stuck on crackers full of bugs. She puts one plate in front of me and one in front of Jack.

"Triple Force," Jack whispers.

"Grandma," I say. "What is that?"

"Kosher sausage and olives on multigrain crackers," Grandma says.

Buzz! A timer goes off and Grandma jumps into

the air. "I'll be right back!" she yelps and hurries to the oven. "That's the sour rum cake for dessert tonight."

Jack says with his sound turned down, "I'll give you dessert . . ."

I hoist up one eyebrow. "Sour rum cake? No, thank you."

Grandma puts the cake on the counter to cool. Somebody honks a horn outside.

"Bye, Grandma!" Jack yells. "My ride to soccer

practice is here." He races out the door and tosses his snack to Patches. Patches gobbles it up and gallops inside.

Quick as I can, I flip my crackers and sausage and olives right into Patches's slobbery mouth.

"Lola!"

I whirl around. Uh-oh.

"Didn't you like the snack?" Grandma asks.

I should tell Grandma the truth. She's a whole lot better at singing and telling stories than she is at cooking.

But I don't want her to feel bad. "I did want to eat it. But Patches was hungry."

"Patches is a dog, Lola," Grandma says. "Dogs eat dog food."

"I'm sorry!" I hang my head like a cow chewing on grass. Moo.

"It was kind of you to think of Patches, but growing girls need nutrition. I'll just fix you another one."

"Thank you, Grandma," I say. I hoist a smile right onto my lips. But my lips are heavy as bowls full of mashed potatoes. Which I wish I had some of.

Grandma goes clicking away and before you can say "yuck" she's back with more of the sausage-olive-cracker combos and Patches is back outside.

Ring, ring.

"Oh, that might be my sister, Sophie," Grandma says. "I'll be right back."

I can hear Grandma's voice from the other room. "You don't say? Well I think *blah blah blah . . .*"

Do I have time to run my plate out to the backyard? Nope. Too bad Mom didn't sew me a Dead Man's Fingers pocket.

Then I have a bright idea. I tuck some of the dead fingers in my permission slip pocket. Then I tuck a few more in other pockets. Before you know it, I've stuffed my pockets full of dead fingers and eyeballs.

It's the perfect plan. I'll just empty out my pockets when Grandma isn't looking.

There's only one problem with that.

16. THE ONE PROBLEM WITH THAT

GRANDMA NEVER STOPS WATCHING me. She loves spending time with me and that's why my pockets are stuffed full of dead fingers when it's time to take a bath and get into my PJs.

The only good thing that happened was she took a taster bite of her eggplant parmesan and something went wrong with that recipe.

Which is why we ordered in Chinese food from the Happy Kitchen and we said hi to Martin the delivery guy AGAIN.

"I'm getting used to having the windows open," I tell Grandma at bedtime.

She cuddles right in next to me. "Yes, the country air is so nice."

AWOOOO! Patches is out there howling at the moon.

"That dog . . ." Grandma says.

"He's excited about the moon," I tell her.

"Oh, is that right?"

"Can I let him back in?" Jack calls.

"Yes, you'd better." Grandma sighs.

Pretty soon Patches comes bounding up the stairs.

"PATCHES!" Jack yells. "He's got your dress, Lola. Your special Lola dress!"

"That crazy dog!" Grandma yells.

Patches goes flying down the hallway, and Jack races after him 'cause Jack likes any excuse to go running down the hall.

ZOOM! They fly by. And *PLOP!* A dead man's finger plops right on the carpet.

ZOOM! They race by again. Patches sure is fast.

But not as fast as Grandma. She leaps straight out of my bed and the next time Patches races by, she grabs the Lola dress right out of his mouth.

RRIIPP.

There goes the permission note pocket.

And out comes a whole bunch of crackers and sausages.

"Lola!" Grandma says, looking
at all those crackers
on the ground.

Jack backs away from
my doorway, leaving Patches
to his feast.

My head hangs down like a
piece of rotten fruit on a rotten
fruit tree.

Grandma takes a deep inside-out breath. She
sits on my bed and pats the seat next to her. I wish I
could sit somewhere else, like the South Pole, but I
can't, so I don't.

"So you didn't like the snack?" Grandma asks. Her voice is kind of squeaky.

"No, Grandma. I'm sorry."

Grandma sighs. "It's okay, Lola. I guess I heard all about the wonderful food Granny Coogan made for you and Jack. I wanted to make you delicious food, too."

We sit there for a minute while I try to think of something. "I like it when we go to Gottlieb's," I say. "And Jack does, too."

Grandma smiles and gives me a hug. "They do have wonderful food, don't they?" Then Grandma's face remembers something. "The note from your teacher. With all the hullabaloo, I forgot to read it."

She opens the envelope. She takes out the letter and she reads it. Then she folds it up and puts it back in the envelope.

"What do you think the note says?" Grandma asks me.

"I'm kicked out of school?"

"No." Grandma takes my hand in hers. "Mrs. DeBenedetti called me today. Again."

"She did?"

"Yes, Lola. She told me about the picture."

"So you already know?"

Grandma nods.

"I'm sorry, Grandma," I say. Then I break out into tears. Loads of tears.

"You don't have to tell me you're sorry, Lola," Grandma says. "But you do have to tell Savannah you're sorry, don't you?"

"If I tell her the truth, she'll hate me, Grandma."

"Lola dear, I don't think that's true. It's important to always tell the truth."

"But Mom told me that if you can't say something nice, you shouldn't say anything at all."

For a second Grandma gets huffy-looking again. Huffy and puffy. Then she sighs.

"Lola, let's get you tucked into bed, shall we?"

And Grandma tucks me into bed.

"Would you like to hear a story?" Grandma says.

"About Lola the Chicken?"

"Yes, and about Zelda the Zebra. Once upon a time Zelda the Zebra came galloping to the farm where Lola the Chicken lived. Zelda came all the way from the Serengeti Plain . . ."

"Is that in Brooklyn?"

"No, it's in Africa. Anyway, Zelda trotted onto the farm and she brought with her all kinds of wild grass from the Serengeti Plain. She thought this wild grass was the perfect thing to eat. And she tried to

convince her little friend Lola . . ."

"Not me, the chicken," I say.

"Yes, the chicken. To eat the grass."

"Patches eats grass," Jack says from the floor
where he snuck into my room. He's lying on Patches.

"Well, Lola didn't like the wild grass from the Serengeti Plain, but she was too polite to tell Zelda ..."

"The Zebra," I remind Grandma.

"Yes. One day Zelda discovered the truth. She discovered that Lola the Chicken really did not like the wild grasses of the Serengeti."

"Uh-oh. Did Zelda get heartsick?"

"Well, no. She didn't. Because Zelda was a wise old zebra who should have known that chickens don't eat grass."

Grandma gets out of my bed and kisses me goodnight.

"Come on, boychik," she says to Jack. "Come on, you sausage-eating rascal," she says to Patches.

"Grandma," I say.

Grandma pauses at the door. She looks just like a beautiful old princess. "Yes, Lola, my bubelah?"

"Maybe Zelda the Zebra learned that she was really good at singing and dancing and telling stories."

Grandma laughs. "That could be."

"Grandma?" My voice is drooping along with my eyes. "If the note didn't tell you about the picture, what did it tell you?"

"That she believes you will know just the right way to show Savannah you're sorry. And you're an absolute pleasure to have in her class. Good night, my little chickadee."

"Good night, Grandma," I whisper.

Mrs. D. told us to be problem solvers. But how can I un-mustache Savannah's mom? How can I show Savannah I'm sorry? I could save my allowance

and buy a camera and take another picture of
Savannah's mom and tape it on her desk. I could
draw a picture of her mom, all purple. Purple hair,
purple shoes, purple, purple, *zzz*.

17. FIELD TRIP OF DREAMS

GRANDMA BRINGS ME TO SCHOOL
early. I sit out in the hall while she and Mrs. D. have
a little chat.

When Grandma leaves, she's got a smile on
her face, so I guess she doesn't think I'm a zhlub.
She hugs and kisses me goodbye and wishes me a
wonderful and spectacular field trip.

"But Grandma," I say. "What about Savannah?"

"We have to be problem solvers, don't we, Lola,
dear?"

Fishsticks. Grandma went to Problem Solvers School, too.

I wait and wait for Savannah to walk in, and when she does I run over to her, lickety-split. I just have to get the words out before it's too hard.

Savannah squints at me through her sparkly blue glasses. "HI, LOLA! Only ONE more day until your mom comes home."

I hurry, hurry, hurry my words out. "Savannah, I'm sorry that I did something so bad, and I'm so sorry, I will never ever ever do it again, and what I did was draw on your mom's picture."

Savannah doesn't look like a koala anymore.

And she doesn't sound like a mouse.

She ROARS like a lawnmower. "YOU DID WHAT?"

"I'm sorry," I say. I stick out my leg. "Here. Kick me with your cowboy boot. I'll get stitches and then we'll be even."

Savannah gives me a Death Glare. "I don't want to be even with you, Lola Zuckerman. And to think

that I gave YOU my jelly beans from California." And
Steaming Mad Savannah stomps off.

Amanda Anderson skips in. She gives me an A+
Amanda Anderson apple pie hug.

"Jessie told me the truth about the swings," she
says. "You didn't push her. She pushed you. And

you fell and that's what happened."

"I know!" I say, and those words are big orange balloons.

"But you still shouldn't have been crowding by the swings."

"I know," I say, and those words are flat tires.

"And you have to be nice to Savannah and Jessie," Amanda says. "We all have to be nice. Right?"

"Right," I say, a little bit porcupine and a little bit skunk.

When every single last person gets there, Mrs. D. calls, "It's time to get your partner for the field trip. Remember! You get who you get . . ."

"And you don't get upset!" the class shouts back.

"Normally we go by . . ."

"Alphabetical order," we remind her.

"But today we're going to try something a little different," she says. "Today we're going in reverse alphabetical order."

"That's very unlike you," Jamal says.

"That's crazy talk!" Harvey hollers.

"That's good news for me," Ben Wexler says.

Z. Ding-dong LAST in the alphabet.

Except today.

"Lola, you get to choose your partner first."

There are a whole lot of faces looking at me: I see Amanda's with a smile like pineapples. I see Savannah's looking down at her purple cowboy boots.

Saying you're sorry isn't as good as showing you're sorry.

"I choose Jessie."
Jessie opens her
mouth and closes it,
just like the rainbow trout
I caught when I went fishing with
Grampy Coogan.
Mrs. D. smiles big. "Wonderful!"
Ben Wexler picks Jamal Stevenson and Savannah
Travers picks Amanda Anderson.

We line up, Z to A, and on the way to the Field Trip Bus, Mrs. D. whispers, "You're a peach."

Peaches have pits.

And that's what I have, too. A giant pit. Now that Savannah is partners with Amanda, she has all that time at the farm to tell Amanda about her mustached mom.

Then I'll never be partners with Amanda ever again.

18. OLD JAN MCDONALD

"IT REALLY WAS HER FAULT.

She was stealing our best friend," Jessie growls. "If she hadn't been swinging with Amanda, I wouldn't have been pushing you and you wouldn't have knocked me into Savannah. My mom told my dad I might be scarred for life. For life!"

"I bet you won't," I say. "Just until fifth grade, maybe."

The bus pulls up to Kookamut Farm.

"All right, Gumdrops," Mrs. D. calls out.

"Remember. You are to stick to your partner like . . ."

"Like peanut butter!" everyone yells.

Mrs. D. nods. "Let's head out and learn about farm life!"

Jessie and I are in the first row, so we get off first, followed by Harvey.

"Look at me, I'm a chicken. *Bock, bock.*" Harvey races back and forth, flapping his elbows up and down.

"Stop it, Harvey!" Jessie hollers. "Stop it!"

All the kids get off the bus and Mrs. D. does roll call in case someone jumped out the window. We march through the wide white gate that says "Kookamut Farm" in big red letters.

Inside the gate, we're on a farm with fields and fields. A farmer lady stands on the front porch of the old white farmhouse. She comes down to greet us. She has red apple cheeks and lots of grey hair and wrinkles. She wears a red plaid shirt. She tells us her name is Old McDonald. We all laugh.

"But you can call me Jan," she says. "Follow me, kids."

Old Jan McDonald leads us into a big metal building. Mrs. D. turns to go inside the farmhouse.

"You might miss the life cycle of a plant," I call out to her.

Mrs. D. raises her travel coffee mug in a salute. "Don't worry about me, Lola, dear. This is my tenth year visiting Kookamut Farm."

Old Jan tells us to sit at the table. We each make a name tag and stick them on our shirts. Lemonade and a cup of popcorn are at every place. While we kids snack, Jan talks.

"How many of you have been on a farm?" she asks.

A few kids raise their hands.

"What happens on a farm?"

Jessie raises her hand. "Chickens try to bite you," she says.

"Nooo." Old Jan leans forward to get a better look at Jessie's nametag. "Sorry, forgot my glasses

today. No, Jerry, chickens don't try to bite you."

The class bursts out laughing.

"That's Jessie, not Jerry," I explain.

Jessie says, "Are you sure there wasn't a kid who was bitten by a chicken a few years ago? Named Dustin Chavez?"

"Positively not!" Old Jan says. "How many of you know about the life cycle of a plant?"

I shoot my hand into the air so fast that Jessie, next to me, says, "Whoa."

But Old Jan McDonald isn't even looking in my direction. I know why, too. Why look over here, in the troublemaker section? Why, when you could look over there, in the nice-kids section? I hope Savannah isn't warming up to tell Amanda about her mom's picture.

"That's okay, because I'm going to teach you," Old Jan McDonald says. She takes out a pencil and draws the life cycle of a green bean on a big piece

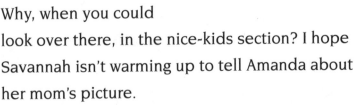

PLANT LIFE CYCLE

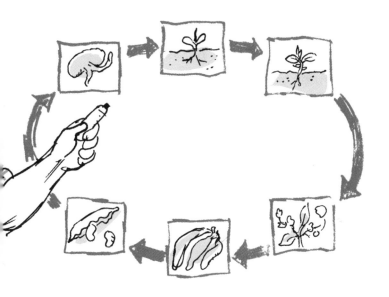

of white paper taped to the wall. Old Jan McDonald
hands out paper and colored pencils and we draw
our own life cycle of a plant.

Jamal tells Old Jan about how plants can take
photos. Or something.

"What season are we in?" Old Jan McDonald asks.

Amanda raises her hand, nice and polite. "It's fall and also autumn."

"Yes! Now it's fall on the farm, so today we're going to let you do a little harvesting! Has anyone ever harvested vegetables before?"

My hand shoots up.

"Yes," Old Jan squints at my nametag. "Lulu?"

The class snickers.

"I'm Lola," I say over the giggles. "And I've harvested raspberries with my Granny Coogan. And tomatoes, lettuce, cucumbers, peppers—" I think for a second. "And with my other Grandma I harvested turnips, carrots, and eggplants, and one zucchini. But it was kind of shrunken up."

"Well, that's wonderful," Old Jan says. "Here." She gives me a stack of buckets. "Give everyone in your class a bucket, won't you, dear? We're going to pick our last crop of beans."

I'm about to pass out the buckets when I trip on Jessie's foot. I stumble and my hands fly out and the buckets go EVERYWHERE!

"You tripped me, Jessie Chavez!" I yell.

Jessie is laughing at me, hard. *HAR HAR*, she laughs.

The whole class starts laughing.

The only person not laughing at me is me. Oh, no, I'm not laughing. I'm crackling. Zinging. Everything that sounds like mad, I am that. But I look over to Savannah and say real loud, "That's okay, Jessie. Accidents happen. I forgive you." I smile with all my teeth at Savannah. She's too busy whispering in Amanda's ear. What is she telling her?

19. CHICKEN TEETH

"I SWEAR ON MY DOG'S LIFE I
didn't trip you," Jessie says.

"You don't even have a dog, Jessie Chavez."

"If I did, I'd swear on it."

"If you did, it would probably be a mean old hound dog that tripped other dogs."

"No way. I'd get a nice dog. A yellow dog."

We are out in the garden, picking beans. Jessie and I work together. Even though Jessie is a mean ol' shover-tripper, she is still my partner. After our class fills up our buckets, we get to stop.

"All right, little farmers!" Old Jan McDonald cries. "A wonderful job! Now, do you know what's next?"

"We're going to visit the animals!" Ari Shapiro calls.

Jessie shoots up her hand. "I'm not done yet. I don't think I did it right. I have to start over."

"That's enough, Jenny," Old Jan says sternly. "Now, I don't like to be Mrs. Tough Guy, but that will be quite enough from your team."

"Thanks, Jessie," I hiss.

"I wasn't trying to get us in trouble."

After we've handed in our beans for Old Jan to bag up so we can take them home, she calls us into a group.

"All right, little farmers, the goats are just dying to meet you!" Old Jan calls out.

I crowd up next to Savannah and Amanda to see the goats.

Everyone gets to feed the goats some special

goat food. I tap Savannah on the shoulder. "Would you like my goat food?" I ask her.

But she and Amanda are singing, "Goat goat goat, goat goat goat, goaty all the way. Oh what fun it is to have a stinky goat today!"

Next come the cows. The cows stare at everyone with big brown eyes.

After we've given the cows a nice long visit, Old Jan McDonald says, "Now the chickens. Follow me."

Timo Toivonen and Ari Shapiro lead the way, followed by Amanda and Savannah, who are holding hands and skipping. But not Jessie. She's squatting on the ground.

"Come on, Jessie," I say. "Everybody's going."

Jessie is staring at an anthill. "Do you think bugs get scared of other bugs?"

"No."

"Do you think they bite each other?"

I strain my neck. I can just see the class turning down a path.

"Hurry up, Jessie. You're going to get us lost." I grab Jessie by the arm. "Get up."

Jessie's lips squeeze together.

She stares at the ground. I squat down to get a better look. I don't see anything. Not even an ant or a beetle. *Plop!* Water lands in the dirt. I twist my head so I can see what's going on in Jessie's face. Two fat tears slide right down her nose. *Plop. Plop.* And I haven't even kicked her in the face.

"What's the matter, Jessie?" I say in a honey-pie voice. "Do your stitches hurt?"

"I don't want to get bitten by a chicken."

"I'm sure that chickens don't bite," I say to mean old Jessie Chavez, the world's biggest best-friend stealer.

"How do you know?"

I think about it. "Well, who says they did?"

Jessie wipes her nose on the back of her hand. "My big brother, Dustin."

"So he's been on this field trip before?"

"Yep."

"Well, my brother has, too. And he told me that Mrs. D. would bring chicken poop into our class.

And so that's why I said she had chicken poop in her bag."

"I thought you were trying to be funny. So Amanda would like you best."

I open my mouth to say something. Something like "shut your trap."

"And it's working," Jessie says. "'Cause she likes you best."

"Is that why you've been acting up today? So that Amanda will think you're funny?"

"No." Jessie kicks a pebble. It's okay to kick a pebble. "It's to slow us down from getting to the chickens."

"Well, now we have to speed up," I say.

"Lola? I really am sorry for shoving you by the swings."

"I'm sorry, too," I say for real.

"I feel bad when you and Amanda talk about how great it was on Cherry Tree Lane."

"I feel bad and heartsick when you teach

Amanda the Hand Jive and won't teach it to me."

"That's 'cause I didn't want to share Amanda."

"Now we both have to share her with Savannah," I say. I'm as sad as Patches when he howls at the moon.

"I'm going to teach you the Hand Jive and will

you not hog Amanda all to yourself?"

"Yes," I say fast, before she bosses the nice out of me.

And I remember what Mrs. D. told me. Showing you're sorry might be better than just saying you're sorry. I hold out my hand to Jessie. "Come on," I say. "Let's go find our class."

Jessie and I walk down the dirt path. There are gardens to the left and gardens to the right.

"I'm pretty sure they took a left up here," I say. We take a left. No Old Jan.

"Are you sure?" Jessie says.

"Sure, I'm sure," I say. "Let's keep walking. Kookamut Farm isn't that big."

We keep walking. We pass by a nice little dog behind a fence.

"Here's a dog for you," I say.

"Hi, doggy," Jessie says. She reaches in to pet the dog. The dog jumps up, growling and smiling meanly.

Jessie jumps back, right behind me.

"You bad dog," I

scold through the fence. "Very bad." I've had a lot of practice with Patches. The dog wags his tail at me. "Don't you wag at me, mister. You say you're sorry to my friend."

We keep on walking. Jessie sniffles. "It's okay, Jessie," I say. "That dog can't get you. See? They

keep him and all of their animals fenced up."

"Okay."

But I'm wrong about that.

'Cause right up ahead is a chicken. A giant brown chicken with a red comb on top.

"L-l-l-l-l-Lola . . . l-l-l-l-look," Jessie says. "A wild chicken."

"That's a rooster. He won't hurt you," I say.

"My brother said . . ."

"Never mind him."

I hold tight to Jessie's sweaty hand. "He won't bother us. We'll just walk right by."

Jessie and I are sneaking past the rooster. He turns around and crows loud as a school bell. He flaps his wings and starts to charge Jessie and me.

"Run, Jessie, run!"

But Jessie is stopped like a stop sign and the
rooster is flying up and landing, flying up and
landing and trying to peck her.

"*SHOO*, varmint! Git out of here," I say in a Granny Coogan voice. The rooster must be stone deaf. He keeps flapping and flapping. I grab Jessie's sweaty hand and pull her away. Finally she starts running. We zip past the dog that barked at us. We zoom past the cows.

The rooster is after us!

"Over the fence," I yell.

Jessie and I climb over the fence.

Squelch! Right into the mud.

Way off in the corner a pig comes out of its hut. It squeals.

"Run, Jessie, run!"

We dash across the pig pen, slipping and sliding through the stinky mud.

Jessie trips and grabs me.

BAM!

We both fall down. We get up and jump over another fence, right in front of the chicken coop. Where our class is bunched up. There's that mean ol' rooster, sitting on a fence post like he doesn't have a care in the world. How did he get here before us? He must know a shortcut.

"OH MY!" Old Jan squawks. "What in the name of Percy the Pig happened to you two?"

"We got lost," I say.

"We tried to take a shortcut," Jessie explains.

Old Jan shakes her head. "Mrs. D. is going to holler up a storm when she sees you. You two need to clean up. Pronto! When you return, you can help us feed the chickens. We just met Friendly, our rooster."

"You two are REVOLTING," Gwendolyn Swanson-Carmichael says.

"I want to play in the mud!" Harvey Baxter whines.

"Lola!" Amanda says. She has her arms crossed.

Oh, no! Savannah told her about the photo.

"I didn't mean to do it. Well, I did mean to do it. But I wish I hadn't done it!"

"You meant to fall in the mud?" Amanda asks.

I stare at Amanda. I need a quick fib. "Oh, well, I've always wanted to roll in the mud."

Savannah makes zombie arms. "I'm coming to get you, Mud Monster."

"Does that mean you're not mad at me anymore?" I ask.

"A little. But not a lot. I know you're sorry."

"How do you know?" I ask.

Savannah leans in and whispers, "Because when you finally got to choose first, you picked Jessie, and I know you wanted to pick Amanda."

I grin at Savannah and whisper back, "She knows lots of good songs, right?"

Savannah wrinkles her nose. "Right." And, "PEE-YOO! You and Jessie need to take a bath."

Jessie wipes the mud off her face. So do I.

We look at each other. I feel a little giggle. I let

it out. Jessie snickers. I laugh again, a little cackle.
Jessie too. We're holding our sides and laughing so
hard, we can't stop.

On the other side of the fence, the pig squeals.

"You stink," says Timo
Toivonen. "In Finland, we do
not roll in mud."

20. ZZZZZZZ

THURSDAY NIGHT I LIE IN MY
bed waiting and waiting to not be awake. The
sooner I go to sleep, the sooner I will wake up. And
the sooner I wake up, the sooner I will see Mom.

I already got to see Dad, 'cause he was home
from Singapore and showing Grandma how to
download pictures of Jack and me onto her laptop
after school. He gave me a thousand hugs (even
though I had dried mud all over me) and then he
gave me a great big box of candy and a slingshot

that could put my eye out if I'm not careful. I
showed him my Friend-of-a-Farmer badge.

I was really, really glad to see Dad.

But I have to wait even longer to see Mom.
'Cause she gets in past my bedtime. Past an eleven-
year-old's bedtime, too, and that means you, Jack.

Every time I close my eyes, I think about my
mom's face. I think about her blue eyes and the fact
that she knows how many kisses to hand out.

Then I think about Kookamut Farm. Someday
when I grow up, I might be a farmer. I'll grow apples
and cucumbers and Jack will come and ride the
horses. I'll ride a horse, too. A white one. Or maybe
a zebra.

I fall asleep and I dream that Mom is home,
sitting on my bed. I can smell her lotion for tired
hands and a little whiff of laundry soap. I can hear
her voice.

"I think she grew while I was gone," Mom
whispers. "Is that possible?"

I realize I'm wide awake. But I keep my eyes squeezed shut. I missed Mom when she was gone but now I don't want to talk to her. I want her to talk to me. I want her to miss me so much she wakes me up with a kiss on my forehead, one on each cheek, and one on my nose. But she doesn't.

"Sure it is," Dad whispers. "Mom said the kids ate a lot."

"Really?" Mom whispers.

"I think she figured out how to order Chinese

food in alien territory," Dad whispers with a laugh tucked in it.

I feel Mom's hand on my forehead.

"My little girl," she says quietly.

My eyelids flutter like butterflies.

"Lola?" Mom whispers. "Are you awake?"

I keep them squeezed shut.

Mom leans down and kisses me on my forehead and my cheeks and right on my nose.

I hear Jack's elephant feet pound into my room.

"MOM!" he yells.

I pop my eyes open. Jack grabs Mom with a hug.

"I'm awake!" I yell. "And I grew!"

Mom laughs and tries to hug us both. Dad wraps in there, too, and we're like a big cinnamon roll.

Grandma swishes through my door with her leopard robe and her fuzzy socks and white stuff all over her face and we squeeze her also. And after everyone piles out, I ask Grandma to snuggle with me and tell me one more Lola the Chicken story.

And she does. This one's about Zelda the Zebra and Lola the Chicken going to Paris.

"Can we go to Paris?" I ask Grandma.

"Why, Lola," Grandma says. "You have the best ideas."

21. A GOOD TOMATO

ON FRIDAY I GET TO SCHOOL FIRST.
Mom drives me because I've got a lot to say to Mrs.
D. before school starts. I'm wearing a brand new
Lola dress that's purple with green pockets.

Mrs. D.'s desk is covered with seeds, apples, a
magnifying glass, construction paper, and flowers. It
looks like a scientific experiment. But I'm afraid to
go in there.

Really afraid.

Mrs. D. looks up. Fishsticks! Too late. I can't hide.

"Lola, my dear," Mrs. D. says. "How are you today?"

"Good," I say. "Mom came home last night from California."

"That's wonderful, Lola."

"Mrs. D., I'm very sorry for being a rotten tomato."

Mrs. D. holds out her arms. "Lola, I knew you would find a way to say sorry to Savannah."

"And I'm sorry for sticking my tongue out at her,

too. And falling on Jessie and getting lost on the field trip and landing in mud."

Mrs. D. has a funny look on her face. Like she's trying to hold her breath. She makes a little snorting sound like a horse laughing. "It was a busy week."

"For trouble," I say.

"Sometimes people have bad days, don't they?"

"And bad weeks."

"You got through it, Lola. And now you have two new friends."

"Jessie and Savannah."

Mrs. D. smiles at me and I smile right back at Mrs. D. It's like playing smile tennis. Sam comes running into the room.

"I'm first!" he yells. Then he sees me. "Oh, no, I'm not. You should be called First-But-Not-Least Lola."

That is funny. I laugh.

I take out my notebook and make two lists.

WHY SAVANNAH AND I ARE FRIENDS

We are brave at the Nurse.

She will love her new Lola dress.

We will swing Double Dippers today cause we can take turns with Amanda and Jessie.

We miss our Moms when they're out in California.

We're glad when they come home.

WHY JESSIE AND I ARE FRIENDS

We run faster than roosters.

We stink in the mud.

She'll love her new Lola dress.

We'll never get mad at each other again.

Never ever ever.

Maybe.

THE KIDS IN MRS. DEBENEDETTI'S SECOND GRADE CLASS (ALPHABETICAL ORDER)

Amanda Anderson

Harvey Baxter

Dilly Chang

Jessie Chavez

Abby Frank

Charlie Henderson

Sam Noonan

Sophie Nunez

Olivia O'Donnell

Madison Rogers

Rita Rohan

Ari Shapiro

Ruby Snow

Jamal Stevenson

Gwendolyn Swanson-Carmichael

John Carmine Tabanelli

Timo Toivonen

Savannah Travers

Ben Wexler

Lola Zuckerman

KOOKAMUT FARM POSTCARDS

KOOKAMUT FARM POSTCARDS

Dear Old Jan McDonald,

I'm very sorry for getting lost and dripping mud all over your place. My mom got the mud out of my Lola dress. Sort of.

I never meant to do anything wrong on the trip. I was on my best behavior, but it didn't work out on account of Friendly not taking a liking to Jessie and me.

Old Jan McDonald, maybe I could come back to Kookamut Farm and be your helper? I could help you teach that old Friendly some manners. Cause I taught my dog, Patches, how to shake hands. Do roosters ever shake hands?

Your friend,
Lola Zuckerman

Dear Grandma,

Remember when I came home from the field trip with postcards? Well, here's one for you! See that lady on the front? That's Old Jan McDonald I told you about. See, she wears overalls that have a lot of pockets like my Lola dress, only she keeps seeds in the pockets.

Grandma, I don't think you would like it at the farm very much. There's no place to order in or get your nails done. But I think Zelda the Zebra and Lola the Chicken would love it!

Lots of love,
Your granddaughter Lola
P.S. Say hi to Great-Aunt Sophie

Dear Granny and Grampy Coogan,

Howdy from Kookamut Farm! Well, now I am home. I got seven postcards from there so here's one for you. All the kids got two, but Harvey and Sam didn't want theirs, and Ruby only wanted one. Guess what? I got chased by a rooster on our field trip! I remember you told me that to train chickens you have to give them a treat, just like when we taught Patches to shake hands. Well, would you give me some tips to help me train Friendly? He's Old Jan McDonald's wild rooster. I know I'll need to bring a LOT of treats.

Bye!
Your little Lola Lou

203

Dear Chuncle,

   I know you don't like the countryside where you can't get a decent pizza. But how do you like farms? This is Kookamut Farm, and that's a place where chickens and pigs live. And guess what!? I got lost, just like you and Dad did in the pumpkin patch when you were kids.

   Chuncle, did you know that a chicken can live to be 20 years old? That's old for a chicken and young for an uncle. Can I come visit you again and can we give you another facial and wrap me in toilet paper so that I look like a mummy even when it's not Halloween?

Love,
Your nice niece, Lola

Dear Lola Zuckerman,

Oh, my dear girl! Don't you worry about a thing! Farms are for getting muddy, I will tell you that much. You and all your friends are more than welcome to come back to Kookamut Farm and enjoy all it has to offer. Since it is fall now, and you got a good taste of what it's like on a farm during that season, why don't you ask your teacher or parents to bring you back in the spring? Then you can meet our new lamb and our new foal and probably a bunch of new chicks. You'll see buds on the trees and crocuses and daffodils blooming, plus a lot of other flowers and vegetables just beginning to emerge.

You were wise to run away from our grumpy Gus of a rooster. I can see that you have experience with animals. Oh, and Lola? We named Friendly when he was just a little fellow! We should have named him Rascal!

With fond regards,
Jan McDonald,
Owner,
Kookamut Farm

Dear Granny Coogan,

Thank you for telling me all about how to train a chicken! I told Grandma, and I bet she's so happy to learn all about it. When I come visit you on spring break, can we train some chickens?

Mom and I got a book from the library and it said you should never get mad at a chicken cause they get mad back. And you shouldn't wave your arms around and scream. In case you ever did that.

Can we also ride your horse Lonesome Joe and feed him carrots?

Oh, guess what? Old Jan McDonald forgave me for making a big mess at Kookamut Farm.

Love,
Lola

Dear Amanda,

    Hi from Lola Zuckerman on Cherry Tree Lane.

    I hope you had a very good time at Kookamut Farm.

    Next time we go on a field trip, can I sit with you?

Love,
Lola

SNEAK PREVIEW OF

Last-But-Not-Least

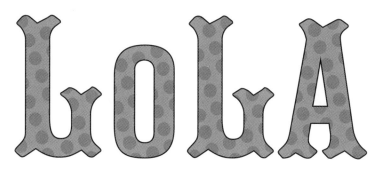

LOLA

AND THE
CUPCAKE
QUEENS

BOOK THREE

1. STINKMANDA AND FUSSY

MY NAME IS LOLA ZUCKERMAN,
and Zuckerman means I'm always last. Just like
zippers, zoom, and zebras. Last. Zilch, zeroes,
and zombies.

ZZZZZZZ when you're too tired to stay awake.
ZZZZZZZZ when a bee is about to sting you. Z. Ding-
dong LAST in the alphabet.

That's a problem when your teacher is in love
with the alphabet. Tomorrow at school, we're going
to share all about our Halloween costumes. By the
time Mrs. D. gets to me, nobody will be listening.
I could say, "I'm going to be a stick of butter," or, "I
think I'll be a lump of dough." Amanda and Jessie will
be playing Miss Mary Mack. Harvey will be hanging
off his chair. Savannah will be daydreaming. That's
when you're wide awake but you're not paying a bit
of attention.

Mrs. D. says we have to be problem solvers. And when she says "we" to me, she means me. But I'm lying here in my bed draining my brain battery out and I can't think of a single good solution.

There's a crack in my wall shaped like a "C." If my name was Lola Cool or Lola Cracker Jack or even Lola Drool, I'd be right near the front of the alphabet. Everyone would be listening up to hear all about my Halloween costume.

"LOLA!" my brother Jack hollers.

"WHA-AT?" I yell.

I whip open my door and *YAAAAAGH!*

Something white jumps out at me.

I take a flying leap back and smack onto my bed. *"AAAGH!"* I scream.

Then I take a second look.

It's just an old sheet.

With an old smelly brother underneath it.

Patches comes running into the room, barking his head off. He jumps onto the bed with me.

"I AM THE GHOST OF ZUCKERMAN MANSION!" Jack calls in his old-movie-scary-voice.

I leap up and whip the sheet off him.

Jack falls on the floor laughing.

"Not funny!" I yell. I sling a pillow right at his not-ghost face.

"Your friends are here," Jack says. "Stinkmanda and Fussy."

"What's going on up there?" Mom calls.

"Nothing, Mom," Jack says. "I just did what you told me."

"Well, come on, Lola!" she yells. "Amanda and Jessie are waiting for you in the kitchen."

I hop off my bed. "Just wait until I tell Mom," I say.

"Oh, really?" Jack says in a squeaker voice. "Did I scare the widdle baby?"

"I'm not a baby."

"*HUNH!*" He jumps at me.

"*ACK!*" I jump back. Then I hurry down the hall.

I keep looking over my shoulder to make sure Jack stays put.

"Hi, Lola!" Amanda says.

"What was all that hollering about?" Jessie asks.

"Jack stubbed his toe." 'Cause I'm not a widdle baby.

Mom gives us some carrots and hummus to snack on, then goes into her sewing room. She's making a brand-new batch of Lola dresses for those people out in California.

Jack zooms into the kitchen. "Oh, look at the cute little kids."

"We're not little kids," I inform him.

Jack pauses above me. "Lola, when was the last time you brushed your hair?" He pokes at my head.

"Stop poking me, you fake-ghost poker!"

Jack pokes me again.

"Is it okay if we take our snack outside?" Amanda asks politely.

"Yeah, let's get away from your brother," Jessie says.

We head into the backyard and sit in a pile of

leaves. Patches lays his head on Jessie's lap.

"You don't get any privacy at your house, do you?" Jessie says. She pats Patches on the head.

"No," I say. "Patches, get off!" But Patches doesn't move. "He likes you!"

"My dog used to be best friends with Patches," Amanda says.

"Now your dog is best friends with my brand-new, super-deluxe, purebred dog," Jessie says. I get a sour feeling in my stomach, like I ate a whole jar full of dill pickles.

"Well, la-di-da," I say. "Patches has a new best friend, too."

"Who?" they both say.

"Savannah's dog," I say.

"I didn't know she had a dog," Amanda says. She frowns. That's when you fold up your forehead. Principal McCoy's face got stuck that way. "What's its name?"

I take a deep breath. "Um . . . Jessie."

"Wait a second. Her dog has the same name as me?" Jessie says. "I don't believe you!"

"It's true," I yelp. I hold up a giant yellow leaf and cover my face with it like it's a mask. Only it doesn't cover the whole thing. I can still see Jessie.

"Who's taking care of Jessie-the-dog while Savannah's visiting Old Sturbridge Village?" Jessie asks.

"Er . . . I am," I say.

"Well, where is she?" Jessie says. She squints at me with laser vision to see if I'm lying.

I get a real sad look on my face. "Jessie ran away. Far away."

"Really?" Amanda sticks out her little finger. "Pinkie-promise?"

"Pinkie-promise," I squeak. "Mom and I put up LOST DOG signs everywhere."

"I guess she's not lying," Jessie says. But Amanda's pinkie is squeezing tight on mine.

"Have you told Savannah yet?" she asks.

"Not yet. I have to go over to her house tonight when she gets home. Or I'll tell her tomorrow at school," I add on.

"She's going to be really mad at you," Jessie says.

"No, she won't," I say. "'Cause we're getting her a brand-new dog!"

Amanda folds her arms across her chest. "Really, Lola?"

"Well . . ." I say, "maybe. If we can't find Jessie."

"You should get her a puppy," Amanda says. "A fluffy little golden retriever."

"Or maybe I'll rescue a dog from the animal shelter," I say.

Amanda claps her hands. "Oh, that's a really good idea!"

"Never mind that," Jessie says. "Look what I've got." She whips a catalog out of a big pocket in her Lola dress. She unfolds it and holds it up.

"World's Deluxe Costumes," I read off the cover.

"Wow!" I'm not *that* excited, but anything's better than talking about Jessie, the Dog That Ran Away (Fingers Crossed) or The New Puppy I'm Getting Savannah (Fingers Crossed Part Two).

Jessie opens up to the center of the catalog.

"Ooh," we three say. Because there they are: The Cupcake Queens. Vanilla Sprinkles, Chocolate Cherry, and Strawberry Sweetie Pie. They have their own TV show, their own book, and their own action figures.

"There's one for each of us," Jessie says.

I look a little closer at the Cupcake Queen costumes. They cost A LOT. I bet Mom and Dad will say no. I told Mom I wanted to be Zero for Halloween because Zero is last and I feel sorry for it. But Mom is too busy running her sewing machine day and night. *Rrrrr. Rrrr.* And go make yourself a snack because you're a big girl.

"And guess what?" Jessie says TV-style. "My mom did the advertising for World's Deluxe

Costumes, so they let her take a bunch of super fantastic costumes! Including the Cupcake Queen costumes!"

We jump up and Patches rolls in the leaves. We yell, "OOGA BOOGA! OOGA! BOOGA! We're the Cupcake Queens!"

Even if that *Cupcake Queens* show is kind of bo-oring.

"But what about Savannah?" Amanda says. "Won't she be sad?"

"Not with a new puppy," Jessie says.

"Yeah, right," I agree, but quiet. Because I wish we could stop talking about the Pretend New Puppy.

"And what about your mom?" Amanda says. "She always makes you a great costume every year."

"Not this year," I say, and "this" stands for all those kids in California who want Lola dresses.

"*Whoooooooooo. WHOOOOOOOOOOOO.*"

The three of us freeze.

"Did you hear that?" I ask.

"Was it Patches?" Amanda whispers.

We look at Patches. He looks back at us and wags his tail.

I peer into the house. Peering is a cross between peeking and fearing.

Mom's inside the kitchen, holding up a big hula hoop. I can just barely see Jack, in his room upstairs.

"Whooooooooooooo. WHOOOOOOOOOOOOOOO."

If it's not Mom and it's not Jack, what is it?